Ben Tucker's truck

and other stories

AZZO REZORI

BOULDER PUBLICATIONS

Library and Archives Canada Cataloguing in Publication

Rezori, Azzo, 1945-, author
Ben Tucker's truck : and other stories / Azzo Rezzori.

ISBN 978-1-927099-93-3 (softcover)

I. Title.

PS8635.E99B46 2017   C813'.6   C2017-906014-7

© 2017 Azzo Rezori

Published by Boulder Publications
Portugal Cove-St. Philip's, Newfoundland and Labrador
www.boulderpublications.ca

Design and layout: Tanya Montini
Editor: Stephanie Porter
Copy editor: Iona Bulgin

Printed in Canada

Excerpts from this publication may be reproduced under licence from Access Copyright, or with the express written permission of Boulder Publications Ltd., or as permitted by law. All rights are otherwise reserved and no part of this publication may be reproduced, stored in a retrieval system, or transmitted in any form or by any means, electronic, mechanical, photocopying, scanning, recording, or otherwise, except as specifically authorized.

We acknowledge the financial support of the Government of Newfoundland and Labrador through the Department of Tourism, Culture and Recreation.

Funded by the Government of Canada | Financé par le gouvernement du Canada | Canadä

Ben Tucker's truck
and other stories

To Brenda

Ben Tucker's truck
and other stories

To Brenda

CONTENTS

Prologue	9
Ben Tucker's truck	13
The visit	21
The funeral	35
Do you love me?	43
The fog	53
Why not?	63
The phone call	71
The dream	79
God loves you	87
To whom it may concern	95
P. S. Dei	103
Dinner at the Kellands	105
Unfinished business	111
The announcement	117
Stella	123
The station master's son	141
News in the harbour	151
The nature workshop	159
An obit	173
The coroner's last case	183
The Dollimonts	193

PROLOGUE

Where to begin? Every story has its own event horizon, and anything on that rim—a paper rose blowing across Mount Carmel Cemetery, a pothole at the bottom of Springdale Street, the foghorn bellowing at Fort Amherst, a bevy of tipsy artists crossing Duckworth Street, a flock of pigeons foraging the subdivision that once was the Ross farm—any of these could be the point of departure and still lead to the place where everything compresses into one ending.

Take the pigeons. Sooner or later they'll shoot over the brow of Kenna's Hill, surf the air currents that move up and down Quidi Vidi Lake, skim the roof of the old stadium where no one skates anymore, and disappear among the stately trees that surround Government House, a grey granite box of a place with a certain stark grandeur. Some of the lieutenant-governors who have lived there were reasonably humble men, but it's not much of a place for pigeons. They're not welcome there, nor a short flight over at the Basilica of St. John the Baptist, which has its own resident dove. So they swoop into the fetid bowl of the harbour, circle the chip wagons, pick their way along the curbs and gutters of Water Street, strut and shit and coo, take off flutter-bluster to perch on the grimy brick ledge of some downtown business, and strut and shit and coo some more.

But no matter how much they dilly here and dally there, the event horizon of a day in the life of a pigeon in this city narrows inexorably toward the container pier at the bottom of the harbour, past the concrete span of the Prince Philip Drive overpass, up the Waterford Valley to the duck pond at the lower end of Bowring Park.

Wings dig in. Air wobbles and twangs. The flock slams into the end of its flight and breaks apart. Every scattering is the end of one story, which, in turn, is but a paper rose blowing along the event horizon of another.

Everyone on the street knew that the old woman at number 35 had died of cancer and that the grinding sadness of her death had also killed something inside the husband she left behind. He broke off all contact with the outside world. Around him and his property grew what one of his neighbours called "the spell"—a barrier of loneliness and neglect as prickly as any hedge of thorns.

Every year, more cracks spread through the pavement of his driveway, more moss and dandelions over the once well-groomed lawn. Maple and aspen seedlings shot up everywhere. Ants invaded the flower beds. More insects came calling than anywhere else in the neighbourhood, more spiders to catch the insects, more birds to swallow the spiders, more cats to swallow the birds. Something had let go. Some will, some order, some program had been pulled, and a long-forgotten savagery had taken over again.

BEN TUCKER'S TRUCK

Alphonsus Doody stood among the gnarled spruce trees that crowded his backyard, dressed in blue overalls over a red and black plaid shirt. He sniffed noisily as he scattered the grain on the ground. The air around him exploded with a flurry of wings.

The snow had gone at last. All over the city, clusters of bladed green were pushing through leaf mould and winter kill. In another few weeks, icebergs would migrate down the coast.

Doody left the pigeons to their feeding frenzy and went inside. Some days he hated the birds because it was Betty who'd started the ritual, and they hadn't noticed or didn't care that she was no longer around. He kept feeding them for her sake, not theirs. Two more weeks, he whispered, as he passed through the back porch and entered the kitchen. And there it was scribbled on the calendar pinned to the wall by the stove: Betty's name, marked under the Thursday column on the second week in May.

The day of her death was now a place as well.

The large photograph above the fold showed a tanker truck on its way to deliver fuel to a small outpost. Down on the waterfront, a fleet of skiffs was forever riding anchor; up on the road, the truck was forever rounding the last bend. It was Ben Tucker's truck, the caption under the picture said so, but it reminded him of Betty. Brave little truck, determined to deliver heat and comfort but never to arrive.

He opened the fridge to crack his first beer of the day. There was none. He swore, grabbed a $20 bill from the tin in the hallway, and left the house for the corner store around the block.

The street opened before him like a story with any number of beginnings. Across the street, Lilly Furlong ducked behind the window through which she kept an eye on the neighbourhood. Three houses farther along, the accountant who'd recently moved in with his young family was lovingly polishing his minivan. At the far end of the street, a boy and a girl ran from one yard to the next, and vanished.

A pale luminescent sky stretched beyond the fences and roofs, the utility poles and bare trees. Betty would have loved it, this silence of lines before the final burst of spring. She'd have enjoyed every moment of it, and he'd have scorned her silently, yet thankfully, knowing that without this scorn he himself was no longer alive.

The cancer that took Betty almost took him as well. He fell apart after she had gone. That surprised, then angered, him. The grinding grief that followed taught him how everything, even life being lived, can come to a standstill. There was a stretch of road between Ben Tucker's truck and the outport as wide and as still as Betty's absence; nothing could change that.

The racket came out of nowhere: a screeching of brakes, a splinter-filled thud, an engine roaring, tires squealing. He caught the fleeing image of a car, a baseball cap worn backwards over a puny face fixed on escape. Then silence.

She lay in the middle of the street, almost peacefully, as if she'd simply given in to the urge to lie down and sleep, young and now broken. Sheer helplessness pulled him to his knees beside her. He knew enough not to touch her but had no idea what else to do.

"Hi," he called softly. "Can you hear me?"

Her eyelids fluttered. She swallowed. A trickle of blood appeared on her lips.

"Don't," he pleaded.

Had she heard him, or was she already deep inside herself—as Betty had been in the final days—beyond the blood on her lips, the injury that had caused it to flow, the pain whose role it was to inform her that she was hurt? He should find help but couldn't tear himself away. He should at least call out but couldn't do that either, because to do so would be to assume that she could no longer hear him.

"You're going to be all right," he whispered. "Do you hear me? You'll be fine."

As if to mock him, her eyelids fluttered again. She groaned. More blood appeared on her lips. The emptiness that had sealed her face was fading. In its place appeared pain. He sobbed because pain, he knew, meant life.

They were no longer alone. A woman had dropped down beside him. She said and did everything he'd wanted to say and do but didn't know how to. Within seconds she'd produced a cellphone and called an ambulance. More people arrived, moved in, offered help. He felt lost and was reminded of how first his family and then the undertaker had taken Betty away from him. He got up and started to leave.

A police cruiser wailed past him and, right on its heels, an ambulance.

"I think this man saw what happened," someone said.

He walked on.

"Sir, excuse me," a voice sang out behind him.

He kept on walking.

"Sir," the voice sang out again.

He felt a tap on his shoulder, cursed under his breath, and turned to face the officer.

They took him to the identification section at police headquarters. He couldn't tell them much about the car. Mid-size, hatchback, dark colour. No idea what make it was. But he did remember the face of the driver, the punk with the hard baby face. He knew the type, the petty criminal who covers the damage done to him with a cold pout, the thing people refer to as a chip on the shoulder. Oh yes, he'd recognize him anywhere, he told the officer. Age 18 to 23, height five three to five six, weight 120 to 140 pounds.

The officer looked up from the keyboard. "We'll give it a try," he said, sighing as he punched in more information. "Please look at the screen."

Had there been only six possible matches, maybe a dozen or two, he might have been able to identify the man. But there were 136. One after another their mug shots flashed by, the misbegotten, mistreated, misunderstood, misguided, mistaken, just plain missed. The beaten for whom survival meant staggering from one knockout to another without a single hug in between. And together they defeated him. The punk at the wheel he thought he would recognize in a heartbeat dissolved like a ghost amid the collective insolence on their faces, the anger in their eyes, the certainty of their resentment and anguish, their self-hatred and self-pity.

He apologized. The officer didn't seem surprised and offered to drive him home. He asked to be dropped off at the corner store. There he made small talk with the owner, bought a six-pack, and walked home.

A few skid marks remained where she'd lain. The sky had turned hazy as if withdrawing in sorrow. He saw himself behind the wheel of Ben Tucker's truck, the forever untravelled road ahead swinging into the cove through the cluster of houses, past the harbour and the fishing stages and the skiffs riding the wind, then curling away from the headland and disappearing over the last hill. It was the truck they were all travelling in. He, Ben Tucker, the hit-and-run driver, the young victim with blood on her lips, the officer who made a living shuffling and dealing mug shots.

Only 14 more days to the anniversary of Betty's death, he reminded himself as he reached his front door. As always, his oldest son would pick him up and take him home for a family dinner. Then they'd all head to the cemetery to spring clean the grave and decorate it with new flowers.

Afterwards, and weather permitting, he'd spend some time sitting on the concrete foundation of the neighbouring grave, where Josh Murphy and his sister Maurcen were laid to rest. He liked to sit there quietly and, with Betty's permission, forget about everything, including her.

―――――――――――

She remembered so clearly the day they moved into their new house on what was then the edge of the city. The place next door was under construction. Across the freshly paved street stretched a row of concrete basements surrounded by gravel and construction trash. There weren't even dandelions around that first spring and summer.

The house received them like strangers. Emptiness stared at her from every bit of bare wall, from every square inch of shiny hardwood floor, from the stark ceilings and the impossibly white cabinets in the kitchen.

"No more fixing leaks like in the old place," Ken had commented approvingly as he inspected the cheerless caverns of the house. "No more fixing," she'd agreed sadly.

It bothered her that from then on he came home the same as he'd left in the morning, in a suit and tie and always at the same time with not a trace on him of what he'd been up to at the office. She missed the smells of his fishing days, the whiff of the open sea, the odour of wharves gone rancid with kerosene and fish guts, the tobacco-drenched comfort of his fishing shed. Now he came home with a halo of stale office air that told her nothing. She had no way of telling what his hands had been on, what he'd walked over, what kind of weather had plagued him. He'd assumed a new form of nothing.

Their new normal, he liked to call it, with a pride she refused to share. Before long she took secretarial courses and got a part-time job as a receptionist. Then it no longer mattered—at least not as much.

THE VISIT

Cora Thornhill was vacuuming the carpet in front of her fireplace when the doorbell rang. She'd slept poorly and was in no mood to speak to anyone.

Who could be calling anyway? The Jehovah's Witnesses had stopped dropping by after Len had died and there was no one left in the house willing to debate them. The usual people collecting for charities had already come and gone. The paper boy still collected his money once a week, but not on Wednesdays. Just a few weeks ago she'd told Bill, the neighbourhood handyman, that there was nothing more she needed done after he'd fixed the latest winter damage to the fence. Whoever was at the door could call another time.

She kept vacuuming. Surely, after all the years, she was entitled to privacy. She'd lived a full life, maybe not as fulfilling as she would have wished, but full all the same. Lately, all she wanted was to withdraw. Her friends had their own reasons for telling her how good she still looked, how sprily she moved for her age, how youthfully she laughed. She knew better. She got up much more slowly these days. The creaking and grinding in her muscles and joints was no longer just a nuisance—it was a genuine obstacle. Something by the name of futility had made a point of waking up with her every morning and hogged her mood for the rest of the day if she didn't say no to it. The silence in the house had become more complex than she ever imagined it could be. More and more she could no longer distinguish between habit and necessity. So much of what had once seemed important had been levelled into flatland, all the whims and urges that had once stood tall as the very essence of what and who she thought she was. Those spring mornings scrubbed with wet snow, the summer garden in which she'd learned to play with life and gotten to know something about the mind of God, the fall mists that had kissed her with a million elfish droplets, the winter nights hard with chimney breath—none of them reached her the way they used to. Whatever power, ability, or innocence that once made her respond without deliberation, without as much as one glance over her shoulder, had vanished, atrophied, whatever.

The bell rang again. She shook her head and sighed, turned off the vacuum cleaner, and went to the door. On the way she passed everything else that still needed to be done: watering the plants, shaking out the rug in the front porch, sorting through the odds and ends that had been piling up on the shelf by the front door again—all the chores she'd come to accept as exclusively hers because there was no one else to pass them on to.

The briefcase that caught her eye told her that the man at the door was an official. She looked into his face for something to recognize, but it was sealed by a thin smile.

She knew instantly that he wasn't welcome, not in her home, not in her life. Ordinarily she would have had no difficulty coming up with a line that sent him back down the driveway before he even realized that he'd been told to get lost. But something about him threw her. Perhaps it was the smile she couldn't decipher, perhaps the absence of himself in his pale blue eyes, perhaps all the other things that seemed to lie buried in the corners of his mouth. She wanted to close the door on him, but everything failed her, and she went blank.

"Cora Thornhill?" he asked.

She nodded.

"Inspector Dunne. Richard Dunne. RCMP."

He produced a business card, which she took, not because she wanted it but because she couldn't think of a way to refuse it.

"Please," he said, pointing toward the living room after he'd entered and taken off his coat.

They sat facing each other across the coffee table. She placed his card between them as if drawing a line. He opened his briefcase.

"I won't take up much of your time," he said, while pulling out a notebook. "But we have new information on your husband's death and would like to talk to you about it."

She should have told him there and then that he was 20 years too late. In 20 years a lot changes. She'd grown old. She'd learned to walk fine lines she didn't even know existed. She'd stopped keeping track of the difference between what she wanted to forget and what she couldn't remember. Len's death had long ceased to be her concern.

"I know it's been many years," he said, as if he'd read her mind. "We can hardly expect you to remember everything. But it's important."

"I may be old, but there's absolutely nothing wrong with my memory," she replied, regaining her composure. "If there's something specific you want to talk about, could you come to the point?"

There was his smile again.

"Can you recall anything your husband might have said about his business trips to Kingston for the Saltfish Corporation that struck you as perhaps a little unusual, out of place?"

"That depends on what you mean by out of place," she replied. She should have said that it was none of his business, that he'd come to the wrong place, Len no longer lived here, had not lived here for many years, and, just to make sure he got the point, neither had his ghost.

He opened his notebook. "And what, may I ask, was your reaction when you heard of your husband's death?"

She remembered the black veil she wore at the funeral. She'd chosen it not to protect her grief but to hide her anger.

"I thought at the time, and I still do, that three bullets, one to the head and two in the chest, is more than what you'd expect from an ordinary robbery, even in Jamaica."

"Possibly. Well, yes."

"You know, I would have been quite able to handle the truth," she said.

"We didn't know the truth then," he replied.

"Oh, I think everyone knew the truth."

He nodded thoughtfully, then leaned forward slightly.

"And how did you know?"

This was the moment to tell him once and for all to get lost. But what was the point? He knew. She knew. They'd all known, Len's family, his friends, his colleagues, yet no one had ever uttered a word. It's the duty of the living to set the dead free—that was what a good wake was supposed to be all about. Instead they'd each added their own handful of silence to Len's death. Perhaps this inspector had his own version of the story or whatever he considered it to be: a case, a file, an argument between him and others. What difference did it make if she told him hers? She'd never told it before. It would be good to get it off her chest. She had a flash of the man's office, his desk, a filing cabinet, a photograph with wife and children, a graduation picture from a police academy showing a younger clone of him.

There was never any evidence as such, she conceded. No letters, no unusual phone calls, no clues in Len's luggage when he came home. But she'd heard it in the stories he used to come back with. There was no way that a man like Len could have noticed the deeper moods of all those limpid mornings or those sweltering middays and liquid sunsets he kept going on about unless he was in love.

"And, believe me, it wasn't me he was in love with. I imagined her dark-skinned and exotic, as you would, with strings of beads hanging all over her place, and a tropical bird strutting around in a metal cage above her bed."

The inspector had stopped writing.

"I think Len wasn't her only lover, and he walked in on her one day with someone else between her legs. And that, I think, is how he ended up dead on the beach. They said it was a robbery. Robbery, my foot!"

The inspector put his pen down and studied her face. "You thought your husband was having an affair?" he asked at last.

Something in his tone made her suddenly acutely aware of her surroundings. The wind had picked up and was sucking away at the corners of the house. Dark clouds with rain-filled bellies were racing through the patch of sky in the window. The furnace kicked in. The inspector got up and walked to the window overlooking the backyard as if he, too, had just rediscovered the rest of the world and its distractions.

Where had his kind been after Len had come back in his box? Where had they been while she'd cleaned out her heart to make room for the strength and will to look after the funeral arrangements, to greet everyone as they arrived for his wake, to put up with it all? No one had had the decency to say something, to let slip even one telltale comment, one raised eyebrow, one knowing smile or snicker, one snippet of the scorn and ridicule she needed to feed the rage howling inside her. They'd patronized her instead with an endless drivel of soothing words and phrases, the kind survivors use to keep a safe distance between the lies of those they've come to bury and their own.

The inspector nodded, gathered his things, and headed toward the front door.

"We just wanted to ask a few questions," he said. "I think you've answered them."

"Well, would you mind telling me what exactly it is I've answered?"

"I'm sorry for your trouble," he said. "We'll be in touch." Then he withdrew behind his smile and left.

She called Steward Bartlett, her lawyer, and told him what had happened. "What do they want?" she demanded. Bartlett promised to make inquiries and get back as quickly as he could.

She pictured herself in a movie, walking up to a little gallery of photographs with their flashbacks set to roll: the scenes of her and Len's courtship on her father's fishing stage, their little big moment at the altar, some of the poignant ups and downs of their childless marriage. She might eventually find her way back into the kitchen and finish pouring that cup of tea and stare through the window into whatever was out there in the dreary June drizzle of the backyard. There'd be several shots of Len's grave with its headstone of red granite and bed of white gravel, and then more of their life together with violins bleeding all over it and clotting into some kind of foreboding.

They'd loved each other once, and she'd never disliked him, even after she'd found him out. He'd been a decent man, too decent at times. Everything had been in order, all his papers, his will, his surprisingly large life insurance. Photographs of him should have been hanging all over the house like those of a lovingly remembered benefactor. His footprints, or whatever it is the dead leave behind, should have been preserved everywhere, from the tools in his workshop to his slippers in the front porch in case they came in handy for a visitor. She'd thrown everything out instead or given it away. Had he drowned at sea like his father, she might have made more of an effort to keep whatever was left of him around. Every fisherman's woman constructs a widow's walk on the roof of her heart, the place she paces when another storm hits and the men's radio voices turn to garble and then to static. That's how she'd lived, how she'd let him go time and again and waited for his return when he was still fishing. She'd been at a certain peace with it, even with imagining him missing in any one of the thousand and one ways the sea swallows sailors and sets their bodies adrift. But no, he had to join the Saltfish Corporation, not because of the steady income, he claimed, but because he wanted to do something more meaningful with his life than just fish.

I know I'll be selling fish we shouldn't be catching to people who'd much rather eat chicken because saltfish reminds them of how poor they are, she remembered him arguing. *But you know, as long as they're poor and we sell them saltfish, we keep something going that protects us too. The moment they're rich enough to eat nothing but chicken, we're at the mercy of rich fish eaters. Now, they're the ones who really don't care. They'll eat fish until there's none left, and when there's none left, they'll move on to something else—alligator, emu, kangaroo, whatever. They don't care that there are still summer fishing camps up in Labrador. They don't even know where Labrador is, for God's sake.*

Of course she should have confronted him with his affair in Kingston much sooner than she had. When she finally got around to it, it was far too late. He simply laughed. How could he? she protested. What was she saying? he demanded, looking genuinely puzzled. Suddenly confused herself, she wanted more than anything to believe in his innocence. She was about to apologize when his mistress flashed through her mind, in bed, provocatively naked, a mocking smile on her full unpainted lips. Who was she? she demanded angrily. He looked at her, no longer laughing, not even smiling, with a dark intensity in which she spotted the full extent of his guilt. She was making things up, he said. Of course she was making things up, she replied. What choice did she have when he refused to tell her what was really going on? Nothing was going on, he insisted. She could see as plainly as if it was written across his forehead that something was. He started giving long speeches about trust. Well, speaking of trust, why couldn't he understand that she wasn't out to find fault with him and brand him an adulterer." She just wanted some honesty. She could handle the truth. There was no truth, he replied. There was always a truth, she countered.

God only knows what tropical heat can do to people, and Len had been talking about it a lot—the films of sweat over every move, the fever of those nights when, as he once described it, his very dreams came oozing out of his sleep into the stifling darkness of the hotel room in which he was staying. When you stew like that day and night, why wouldn't something give, whatever decency you thought you possessed? How can you stay true to yourself when you're in a place that won't let you hold on to who you thought you were? He must have allowed himself to be bewitched. In that case it served him right that this was what his business suits and all that foolishness about saving something that no longer existed brought him to: death by stupidity.

Bartlett called back an hour later. He spoke slowly and carefully as if walking his words on a leash. He'd worked his contacts. There was an investigation. Police were looking into an old connection between Len and a recently infiltrated drug cartel. He was sorry. He had no further details, but they wanted to talk to her again. He suggested a meeting at his office in two days. It was the best he could do.

Cora could only bring herself to nod.

"Are you all right?" Bartlett's voice came through the receiver.

She took a deep breath. "Yes, of course I'm all right. Two o'clock on Thursday afternoon sounds fine. Thanks, Stew." And she hung up.

She had a sudden memory of herself, Len, and a small group of friends and family standing on a wharf in Bay Bulls, purple clouds low and threatening like the lid of a coffin, the bay streaked and flattened by a wind blowing hard and steady off the land. There was wrath in the sky so unmistakable that the safe return of Sean Flaherty and the four young men who'd gone fishing with him would have been nothing short of a miracle. There was no miracle that day.

And then the images changed to an unknown place she'd have to become familiar with now: dark-looking men shouting into walkie-talkies, a plane touching down on a jungle runway, more men coming into view armed with guns, and another group negotiating in a small office, a ceiling fan slicing the sticky heat, bugs crawling everywhere, money and corruption in the air, and in the midst of it all the Len she'd never gotten to know, the Len who might have been able to convince her that his ghost was worth keeping after all.

She slumped into the nearest chair and buried her face in her hands.

"How dare they? How dare they?"

You grew up thinking that the old man knew everything. Now you're left wondering how much he did know, and the only answer you can come up with is, not enough.

As much as you insist that he failed you, in his own way he tried. But you were so caught up in him, everything he said he saw in you, dismissed in you, and sometimes praised in you, was not about you but about him. Only when his powers started to wane did you recognize his offer to consider yourself his equal. You rejected it.

You said he didn't deserve it.

You said, angry at last, how dare he?

You said, one day I'll meet him face to face and stare him down.

But you waited too long. That day never came.

THE FUNERAL

An act of God was how Gary Walsh viewed his father's death, a comeuppance long overdue. He could never understand how some of his aunts and uncles, all decent people, had died the most senseless early deaths by cruel diseases and stupid accidents, while the one genuine prick in the family had been allowed to live as long as he had. What's more, if the diagnosis of angina had been sent him as a warning, his father hadn't just ignored it, he'd made his usual show of it. Well now, he'd liked to crow, the fact that something inside him wasn't functioning properly anymore was no excuse for hobbling around like a cripple. Whatever it was that had kept him going all his life was the only true thing he ever had, and he wasn't about to give it up. Chronic chest pain and discomfort had convinced him to take the medication prescribed by his doctor, but it hadn't been enough to make him change his ways. His family's protests that he was killing himself had had no effect. On the contrary, he said he was doing everything he could to keep living, and he'd deal with dying when the time came, and the more unexpectedly and suddenly the better. Well, God had finally obliged and let him have it.

Gary didn't hear of the death until the day before the funeral. He'd been gone without his cellphone for a week of paintball and white-water rafting on the Rouge River. The message was on the voice mail at his apartment in Montreal. It was Susan: "Dad has died. Please try to come. Funeral is Thursday. One o'clock at Purcell's. Love you."

Susan met him at the bottom of the airport escalator, shaken but happy to see him. He knew she was suffering the most because she'd been daddy's girl.

"So how did he die?" he asked, as they sped down Portugal Cove Road.

"Heart attack. Out of view in the garden," she replied.

"As he would. How's Mom?"

"I'm not sure. There's moments I think she's relieved. Most times she's just very quiet."

"She'll get over it, though at her age you ask yourself what for."

The coffin was to be closed by 12:30 for the service at 1 p.m. They hit every red light and were running late.

"It's OK," Gary said. "They can wait, and I don't suppose the old man is in any rush anymore."

"How long are you staying?" Susan asked.

"A few days."

"You can stay longer. It's different now."

"No, it's not. I'm sorry, but it never will be."

"The kids can't wait to see you. They like you."

"Why wouldn't they? I'm the one in the family who doesn't expect anything from them."

"All I'm saying is, that's history now."

"It's too late for history," he replied.

They made the last intersection just as the light turned red. Susan pulled into the parking lot, killed the engine, and let out a deep sigh.

Everyone was gathered in the lobby. Gary looked for his mother and saw her standing by the door to the chapel. She did not return his embrace.

"Hurry!" she said.

He'd forgotten how much his father had shrunk in old age. He was laid out in an ill-fitting suit which diminished him even further. His stubby-fingered hands rested on his collapsed belly like two fatally entangled spiders. Death and the makeup job had given him a gruesome dignity as if he was on loan from a wax museum. Gary searched his heart for sorrow. All he found was self-pity.

Don't whine, his father's ghost hissed. *Don't snivel. Don't eat your worms in front of me. If you want something from me, don't expect me to come looking for you in your pathetic little corner. Meet me out in the open.*

You know as well as I, there's no open and never was, Gary replied. *What you called the open was your own corner. You insisted that it was the family's common room. It wasn't.*

This is rubbish. I owe you nothing. What do you want from

me? And the corpse had him there, because to speak the truth was to humiliate himself and ask for love.

"I don't want anything from you," Gary said out loud. "Let's face it, you have nothing more to give." He suppressed the messy feelings he felt rising inside him, turned, and left.

The funeral procession crawled along LeMarchant Road, led by the hearse with its cadaverous blue light flashing like an alert for grave robbers. Gary and his mother sat as far apart as the rear seat of the limousine allowed. He knew she believed and insisted on believing that he'd hated his father. He would have loved to. Hate would have been so much easier than the emotional no man's land that had stretched between him and the old man, the emotional trench life of a stalemate with its sporadic, usually pointless, and always utterly destructive outbursts of violence.

No, he hadn't hated his father, he simply hadn't been able to forgive him. A therapist once tried to pry out of him what exactly there was to forgive. "Everything," he'd replied. "Everything?" the therapist had asked. Gary had promptly discontinued the sessions. Still, the therapist had been right. *Everything* wasn't the correct answer, though it wasn't far from the truth either. There was everything his father had dismissed, which was far too much. There was everything he'd accepted, which was far too little but always served to protect his self-interests. There was everything he'd done to make sure he was always right and always had the last word. And there was everything Gary himself had had to swallow for no better reason than that he was young and innocent and utterly browbeaten.

As they passed the Village Mall on the way to the cemetery, his mother turned to face him.

"Did I ever tell you how your father and I met?" she asked.

"No, you never. And I don't think we ever asked."

"That's right, you never did."

Gary waited for his mother to start telling the story, but she'd fallen silent again.

"You know, Susan and I used to spend hours making up our own versions of the story. Mine was that he let you chase him, Susan's that he made the moves. I liked hers better. She imagined that you were really an orphan and he rescued you."

A little smile spread across his mother's face and stayed there until the limousine stopped at a red light. Then it vanished. She looked out the window, almost in a panic.

"He was a very selfish man," she said, her voice trembling. "I'm sorry. I really am sorry. But you know, he had his own issues." And she went on about a Sunday drive with his father a few weeks before his heart attack. They'd taken the Trans-Canada Highway and turned onto Witless Bay Line. He'd been rambling on about what was real and what wasn't, a favourite topic when he was in an expansive mood and felt the urge to have important thoughts. She'd stopped listening and let her mind wander when a shift in his tone caught her attention. He was talking about events at a lumber camp, a fire and the search for bodies in the ashes. It took her a while to figure out that it was the story of his own father's death and double life as a dependable and loyal employee in the camps and a vicious drunk at home. One part of her listened with horror and felt truly sorry, the other kept a cool distance, thinking it was all much too late and a pathetic way to ask for forgiveness. He talked about his own confusion as a boy and a young man, and his long search for something to believe in. Finding nothing, he built a wall around the emptiness inside, then a dungeon, then the whole vanity of a castle. There he ruled, a king to the outside world, a warden to the nothing inside.

Gary's mother stopped, shrugged sadly and apologetically, and then started to cry. She continued to cry until they reached the cemetery.

Gary walked around the limousine and opened her door. He waited while she dried her eyes and blew her nose. Then he leaned forward and offered her his arm.

"Wait for Uncle Martin," she said, as she straightened up, spotting Susan coming across the parking lot. "I'm OK. I'll walk with Susan."

Gary watched the two walk toward the tent set up over the grave. He heard his father laugh as he used to, his head thrown back, his chest stuck out, his whole body shaking with self-indulgent contempt as he made it perfectly clear that the funniest thing of all was how little he gave a damn.

Gary closed his eyes and waited until the laughter faded. It seemed to take forever. When he looked again, Susan and his mother had already blended in with the crowd at the gravesite. A second group of mourners moved slowly and quietly past him. Uncle Martin was not among them. It occurred to him that this was his chance to escape. He took a deep breath, dismissed the sob that had started to cramp up his chest, and followed.

They met on a Saturday night on George Street. She was part of a group which had somehow bumped into his. They ended up next to each other at the bar. She barely reached to his shoulders, small with black hair and startling blue eyes. There was something both quick and melancholic about her which told him that the usual bullshit would get him nowhere.

She took him back to her place on the fifth floor of her apartment building. All the way up he felt he was being tested—by the blank stare of the lobby, the brawling odours in the elevator, the ghosts of past meals hanging out in the hallway.

He remembered a story in Arabian Nights about a golden bird on top of a magic mountain and invisible voices distracting those trying to get to it. Here he was now, climbing without the slightest idea what besides her bed the mountain had to offer and wondering what whispering mysteries he was passing and missing on the way.

A flock of pigeons came to roost on the balcony that night, crooning like a crazy band of mariachi, cooing and shuffling and stirring up darkness while he and Lynn drifted off.

DO YOU LOVE ME?

"We're first again," Gerry Parsons complained, as he entered the apartment carrying the dish of meatballs he was famous for on the potluck circuit across town.

"Oh, stop grumbling," said his wife, Marianne, coming up behind him with her equally popular apple cheesecake.

Lynn rushed to meet them while telling Sean to check the ribs and the wings in the oven.

Ben Knight arrived next with his usual bachelor contribution of nacho chips and salsa he had bought at a convenience store on the way. Tom Barrett brought his Greek salad from long ago when he'd courted Laura, his wife, on a Greek island. Claire O'Connor arrived with her latest vegan creation and what Ben described as her Hera complex—her need to be everything to everyone because she was so capable and yet so insecure.

"This is Greg," Claire said, pointing at the man at her side who was carrying a dish covered with tinfoil. "Greg, this is everyone."

Greg smiled pleasantly and openly into the room. He was the standard issue of tall and handsome, probably a few years younger than Claire, with full auburn hair, hazel eyes, and an air of innocence that, at his age, suggested an uncomplicated intellect. Lynn was just about to lead the two into the kitchen when Maisie Bishop turned up.

"I'm not sure about this, not sure at all," Maisie said, as she handed her casserole to Lynn. "I had it at Hilda's the other day, and I liked it so much I asked her for the recipe. But it doesn't look and smell anything like it should. You don't have to eat it."

"Don't be silly," said Lynn, lifting the dish to her nose and sniffing it loudly. "It smells absolutely delicious."

"No, I didn't really have time to do it properly," Maisie insisted. "Mother called from Gander and said she wasn't feeling well again. I don't know what to think. You know how she goes on. I can never tell if she's really sick or just looking for attention."

Claire, who stood nearby, laughed. "Mothers will do anything to get attention."

She should know, Sean thought. He'd seen Claire with her own children, the boy and the girl from her broken marriage. He'd always admired the way she had them under control, but one day they would go their own way and eat meat and swear openly, and everything she'd tried to do for them would be undone the way she'd probably undone her own mother's work. He caught her looking sharply at Greg, whose eyes were wandering over Maisie's breasts. Mothers are like sculptors who never get to finish what they've started. No wonder they can't let go. If Greg gets to stick around long enough, he'll wave the children goodbye one day with a stepfatherly see-you-later, but Claire will complain endlessly that they're not calling home enough, and she'll never understand that she can't let go because she sees them as incomplete and as always belonging in her studio of motherhood.

Barb Mitchell arrived with a huge pan of lasagna which, she announced, needed to go back in the oven for another 10 minutes. Sean took the pan, and she followed him into the kitchen.

"Peter isn't coming," she said.
"Oh? What's his problem?"
"I'm his problem." Barb laughed bitterly.
"What happened?"
"You wouldn't believe it."

Barb was an urban planner by profession, but she often said that if she had her time over, she'd choose alternative healing. Her most striking trait was a deep and endlessly probing cynicism. Her marriage had been a disaster. Years later, she was still struggling to recover. What kept her going was her irrepressible lust for life, but it was tough going with recurring bouts of depression which she herself admitted bordered on insanity. She had enormous survival skills; she had equally enormous blind spots out of which she constantly ended up side-swiping herself. And she was always, and always desperately, looking for a man.

She and Peter, an electrical engineering instructor at one of the local trade colleges, had seduced each other at the last potluck. It was a mistake, she admitted, but it took her a week to find out. A good week, mind you. A very good week. He was a lovely man, but maybe she was too strong for him, and he couldn't take that. Good sex, yes. A bit kinky, but neither of them minded. He strutted too much though, put too much effort into proving that he was an iron man with a soft heart. She thought at first he just needed more time to find his comfort zone, and, frankly, she got off on the tension. But he never made it past being a little boy playing games to see how far he could push. They reached the moment of truth one morning at breakfast. He complained that she'd let the toast burn. All of a sudden her father and her former husband stood over her, running her down, telling her how absurd she was despite all the new-age personality building she was putting herself through. She lost it. After all, he wasn't exactly a completed piece of work either. He took it, well, not very maturely. He was far more spoiled and insecure than he'd let on. She told him to get lost.

"Men are pigs," she said, "but they don't want to admit it. They blame it on women instead."

"Off with their tails," Sean declared.

"Well, maybe not," Barb replied, and left to join the crowd in the living room.

The party was in full swing. Sean had a long chat with Bruce Porter, who'd recently made the pilgrimage to Santiago de Compostela. He smoked a joint in the spare bedroom with Ben and Maisie. He listened in on Marianne and Alice Doyle engage in a mind-bending conversation about Jesus, Mary Magdalene, and the songs of Leonard Cohen. He joined a crowd around Tom and Claire, who were going at each other again—Claire not willing to accept that her smarts were no match for Tom's sheer bullheadedness. Someone he'd never met before and who introduced himself as Mike dragged him off into his life of petty frustrations deep inside Confederation Building.

Sean excused himself and made his way to the kitchen to be alone. Maisie stopped him before he got there.

"I've been watching Lynn. I can't take my eyes off her. She's amazing," she said.

"I agree," Sean replied.

"Are you two happy?"

"Well, what's happy?"

"Oh, come on. Why can't guys ever give a straight answer to simple questions of the heart?"

"I didn't know happiness was a simple question."

"No, I suppose you wouldn't." Maisie sighed, and left.

He moved into the empty kitchen, closed his eyes, and listened for Lynn's voice but couldn't make it out among all the noise. He missed her. She'd told him shortly after they first met that she was an adopted child. Later she admitted she'd made up the story but insisted it was essentially the truth. All her childhood she'd felt like a stranger in her own family. Her father was a successful businessman, a man of impeccable respectability in public but a nasty drunk at home. Her mother was a bitch and drove her father to drink in the first place. They'd sinned against each other from day one but were too hung up on convention to put the only reasonable end to it. There was no love in the house. Lynn moved out when she was 16, and now her friends were her family, and that's how she wanted it.

Oh yes. Love. Lynn never tired of telling him how much she loved him. It was also her bottom line whenever they'd argued their way into another dead end and she needed a way out. She said he had no idea how much she loved him. It was tempting to ask her what exactly she meant by love, but that was asking for trouble. The presence of love could be discussed, the absence of it even more, but not love itself. Love, she insisted, was its own proof. And that was the difference between her and him. Her love was immune like faith, it soared even when war raged below. His slogged through the mud of conflict like a shell-shocked soldier, high on reprieve one moment, back in the trenches of despair the next.

Lynn entered the kitchen. "Oh, there you are!" she exclaimed, surrounded by a lovely halo of tipsiness. "Why are you in here?"

"I don't know. I guess I got lost."

"Well, come on out. We won't bite."

He followed her back into the party, and before he knew it the fog of solitude had lifted. After two more drinks he started to float. He had another toke, this time with Ben and Greg, and then it all became a big blur, and he was happy.

It was over far too soon. Claire and Greg left first. As if the rest had all been waiting for the signal, everyone was suddenly chanting their goodbyes and good nights. It had been a lovely party. Thanks a lot. No, thanks a million. Oh, go on! See you on

Monday. Yes, I have my dish. Thanks again. Good night. Sleep well. Good night.

Lynn was drunk. She put on her favourite album by Joni Mitchell and began to dance. Sean smiled and turned to walk back into the kitchen and start putting things away, but she followed him and tried to pull him into what had opened up inside her. He recognized it as the place where she wanted him but where he really wasn't allowed except as a wish, that river of her own she liked to skate away on. He also knew she couldn't have him there unless he agreed to be devoured.

She insisted, pushing and pulling him with increasing impatience as if he was withholding something that belonged to her. He wanted to shout, *Stop! Don't you see?*, but she was beyond hearing range. She was dancing to herself with an inward look which told him that the only way to reach her now was to follow unconditionally, and that he couldn't and wouldn't do.

She stopped abruptly, walked over to the stereo, turned it off angrily, and disappeared into the bedroom.

"I need some fresh air," he announced loudly and left the apartment.

She was asleep by the time he returned. He climbed into bed, hoping not to awaken her, and settled his head on the pillow. She stirred.

"I'm sorry," she whispered.

"It's OK," he lied.

"Are you angry with me?"

"No, I'm not," he lied again.

He listened as her breathing slowed down. He lay there for what seemed like a long time thinking of love and how it kept confusing both of them.

She stirred again.

"Will you always love me?"

"I will."

She fell asleep again. He gave himself over to the drowsiness that had begun to descend on him, and saw her there, on her pond, all alone but carefree and happy, her skates biting into the black ice.

He adjusted the mirrors of the bathroom cabinet until he saw himself reflected again and again to the nowhere of infinity.

The faces stared him down silently.

"Spectre," he mumbled. "You scrutinize this face behind which I stand confused. You ape me aping you and fake eternity where your parallel meets mine."

The faces told him that he needed a shave. He heard Ruth moving in the bedroom, fumbling her way out of sleep.

"Fine," he replied. "I shall turn again and feel your dark side in my back and, blind to the day, grope toward another night, when wind-chilled windows die from outside and cast, once more, your image."

Ruth knocked on the door. "Jeff! Will you be much longer?"

THE FOG

Tripped by the seven, the alarm shrilled into her dream. She groped through the mist of awakening for the touch of metal she knew housed the racket. She tried to focus on her fumbling fingers, but there was far too much distance and confusion. With a reflex of defeat she closed her entire hand. Something yielded and locked, and there was silence. She floated, and then remembered that Steve wasn't there.

Slowly and still dripping with sleep, the day ahead emerged—the office, lunch alone, the office again, the evening alone again unless she went drinking on George Street.

She hadn't heard from Steve for five days. He'd left a note on the kitchen table: *I'll be back*. No hugs, no kisses. Looking for him had gotten her nowhere. He'd gone underground.

She gave herself longer than she needed for the walk downtown because she craved fresh air. More than that, she craved time, empty time like a glass of clear water, or better yet, like nothing at all. The wind had shifted onshore. A bank of fog had piled up outside the Narrows and was getting ready to spill into the harbour. The temperature dropped street by street. She was chilled by the time she reached Water Street.

She hoped he might have left a message on her office line. He hadn't. It was all so humiliating because she should have seen it coming. He'd been acting up again, playing games, being rude and inconsiderate, thinking of nothing but himself. And as usual she'd put it down to the immaturity she still couldn't bring herself to hold against him.

The morning passed quickly. She declined an invitation by two colleagues to have lunch with them and left on her own shortly after.

Water Street had drowned in fog. Neon signs flashed and floated in nowhere. People appeared and disappeared like spirits floating in and out of adjacent worlds. Ghostly cars glided by with large dead eyes. Into and through it all the Fort Amherst foghorn moaned in a strange near distance. It reminded her of a beast locked in a closet and dying of loneliness.

She walked on until she found the greasy spoon she and Steve used to frequent in the early days. The place was packed. The owner, a tiny Chinese matriarch, gave her a surprised but friendly smile. She picked the only empty table left.

The air was thick with the smell of damp clothes, the clatter of dishes, the hissing of grease, the clinking of forks and knives. Two middle-aged women at the table next to hers—office workers like her, she guessed—were picking away at salads.

Three businessmen at a table next to them were trying to get the attention of the waitress. A little boy and his older sister were devouring French fries while their parents were deep in conversation. An elderly couple got up and left. A plate exploded in the kitchen, followed by laughter.

She saw herself starting a whole new life. She might get to know the girl and her brother well enough to have a good idea what to get them for Christmas and their birthdays. She might discover which of the three businessmen could be trusted the most. She might stop the elderly couple and ask them what love has meant to them. She might ask the waitress, who took her order for spring rolls and a small garden salad, the same question. Love? the woman might answer. Don't be talking! The first man ditched her after he got what he wanted. The second one wanted to ditch her but couldn't do it, so she had to do it for him. The third one had a history like hers, so they got married, which meant that when the time came to split, things got very messy. She was still waiting for Mr. Right. She'd probably served him at the restaurant and never knew it. He had a wife and family in Houston or Stavanger. Just her luck.

She let her mind drift back to the Halifax waterfront where she and Steve first met. She was living on a small freighter whose cabins the owner had put up for rent until he'd scraped together enough money to make the old tub seaworthy again. She was one of five tenants, all young and rootless like her. The toilet had to be flushed with harbour water hauled up by bucket. The gulls mewled and shrieked all day and half the night. Steve had stood there on the wharf one evening carrying a harp. He was from Vancouver, he said. His Irish blood was calling him east. He mumbled a few words she couldn't understand. He said they were Gaelic. Did he speak Gaelic? she'd asked stupidly. No, but it was in his blood, like the music he played on his harp. She laughed, but he stood his ground. She thought it was all rather charming, and they became friends.

She introduced him to the owner of the freighter, who had plans to set sail for Ireland the following spring and agreed to take Steve on as a deckhand. Winter arrived. Living on the unheated tub became unbearable. She left and worked her way down the Eastern seaboard all the way to Georgia, where she landed a job as a gofer on a golf course. She sent him two postcards. He replied to the second. The work on the freighter was painfully slow, but the plan was still to sail in spring. She got another card in February. His spirits were low. He was stuck without money and without passage to Ireland. The tub had been sold for scrap. The owner was a scoundrel.

She returned to Halifax in June. The harbourfront was changing. The old wharves were giving way to redevelopment. Many of her friends had scattered. She felt lonely and decided to go home to St. John's. On her last day in Halifax she ran into him. He was living with three other young men in an apartment two streets up from the harbour. He invited her over for supper. They put on a party which unfolded with such ease that she realized they'd been partying every night. There was a barrel of homemade beer. Dozens of people turned up. They drank a lot and rolled a lot of joints. He told her he'd sold his harp to someone who needed it more than he did. He'd learned at least that much, that he'd never make it through life with a harp. There was no more talk of Gaelic, no talk of returning to Vancouver either. He'd turned to Canada Manpower for help, and they'd put him through a retail training course. She told him he needed to get out, move on. He agreed. She asked him to come with her to Newfoundland. He accepted.

They took the bus. She watched him closely as they left the forested regions of the island and entered the boulder-strewn barrens of the Avalon Peninsula. He said he felt he wasn't sure what to make of it but couldn't wait to see what was next. She was happy for him. It was then that she fell in love with him.

Her family thought he was a complete flake even without his harp. But he proved them wrong. He landed a job at a shoe store at the Avalon Mall. Within three years he was the regional manager for all the company's stores across the province. By that time, they'd already moved in together.

And now he was gone again. On the Sunday before he disappeared they'd driven to the top of Signal Hill to look at the iceberg that had run aground just off Fort Amherst, a stranded chunk of northern enamel giving off a cold and eerie beauty which made her think of outer space.

"Poor thing," Steve had observed. "It's trapped."

She'd been looking out over the open ocean where dozens of other icebergs were drifting south like scattered members of a vast herd of ocean-grazing beasts. "I'm sure it's exactly where it's meant to be," she'd pointed out.

"Well, that's easy for you to say. You're not it."

"And you are?"

He'd shrugged. "I guess it'll melt until there's nothing left."

"Nothing left?"

He'd dodged the question by taking a sudden interest in a fishing vessel rounding the iceberg to reach the harbour. She hated his insincerity, his display of mock indifference whenever she caught him out.

"So that's you down there?"

"Who knows?"

She'd seethed with anger for the rest of that day. After all those years, and after all the times he'd gone missing before and come crawling back, he was still accusing her of having trapped him.

Another customer entered the restaurant. For a moment she thought it was Steve. He was about the same age and of roughly the same build, slim but not athletic, pale by nature. But that was as far as the resemblance went. He was a completely different type, darker but also softer. He brushed his damp hair off his forehead and seated himself at the table left empty by the elderly couple. He had a brief conversation with the waitress, who left and came back shortly with a cup of coffee. Then he looked around as if to confirm from a great distance that he was where he meant to be. He unfolded a newspaper and withdrew behind it.

She couldn't take her eyes off him. She imagined contacting him through a personal ad in the paper. He'd have to like reading books and listening to music and walking on beaches, not because those were her favourite activities but as a safeguard against coarseness. He'd have to be able to stand his ground without turning it into a fight. And he'd have to know when to be the slave and when the master. She imagined discussing Steve with him and what had made him walk out on her again.

"So he left because he feels that you've become his keeper?" she had him ask.

"He says I have."

"He feels trapped then?"

"I don't know. He keeps coming back."

"Men who keep coming back are fools," he replies too glibly.

"No, they're not. Perhaps they can't help themselves."

"You mean they're to be pitied rather than loved?"

She had them start over.

"So you've become his keeper?"

"Yes, I have."

"And whose decision was that?"

"We didn't plan it that way. It just happened."

"Things like that don't just happen," he states. "No man will be kept willingly."

"He loves me then?"

"Maybe. Men want to be good lovers, but they must be undone first. Women offer them that opportunity, but most men refuse to take it. So they end up trapping themselves."

She watched him as he folded the paper, put it on the table, produced a pen, and started doing the crossword puzzle. It finally occurred to her that he was waiting for someone. A friend? A business partner?

Another group of customers paid and left. More people arrived. He looked up suddenly, and a wide smile split his face. She fumbled for her coffee, almost knocking it over. What struck her most about the woman who walked by was how unlike her she was. Better looking, there was no doubt about that. Taller. More self-assured. A woman who made heads turn and knew it. But just as quickly she spotted something hard and demanding. She felt the envy inside her turn to triumph.

She leaned back in her chair and observed the silence between the two. It was a silence that could only have grown from a devastating familiarity, the kind that had never existed between her and Steve because he wouldn't allow it. She felt a chill as if the woman had brought in the fog with her. She drank up and paid.

She had some time left before she was due back at the office and decided to take a detour along the waterfront. Somewhere on Water Street Steve was probably even now performing for the benefit of some friend or stranger in the steaming cave of a bar, pretending to be free. Impulsively she opened her handbag, rummaging through it for something that belonged to him. At the bottom she found a little key on a silver chain he'd given her years before, claiming it was the key to his heart. Corny but cute, she'd thought. She'd even worn it for a while.

She walked to the edge of the harbour apron and stopped next to the squat mushroom shape of a bollard. Above her loomed the fog-blurred bow of a large ship. The rope that ran up to it slackened and tightened like the breathing of a slumbering giant. The foghorn spilled its mournful voice, and a wave of sorrow washed over her.

She felt her knees buckle. Panicking, she raised her hand and flung the necklace into the fog. It seemed like ages before she heard a tiny splash.

"Get better first," her mother said. "Then we'll talk."
"Fine," she replied. "Don't bother then."
"No, no," her mother protested. "That's not what I meant."
"Well, what did you mean?"
"I meant it's hard to talk to you when you're so angry."
"And you're not?"

WHY NOT?

Her mother's voice met her halfway down the stairs.

"You'll be late."

Kim wasn't even close to being late. She had at least another half hour before Jamie was due to pick her up. Half an hour alone with her mother wasn't late, it was an eternity.

Kim entered the kitchen. Her mother was putting away dishes. "Will you be home for lunch?" she demanded, her voice hard from the quarrel they'd had the night before. *Let it be*, Kim told herself as she dumped cereal into her bowl.

"Hello?" her mother insisted.

Here come the arched eyebrows again.

"I'm not sure," Kim replied as flatly as she could.

She poured milk over the cereal and seated herself at the kitchen table. Her mother had started wiping down the counter by the sink, her lips squeezed tight. This was supposed to be the new start they'd agreed on after their last visit to Dr. Spencer.

"I think Jamie and I'll have lunch together," Kim said to break the silence. Bringing her boyfriend into the picture always worked.

Her mother turned, all smiles now.

"I think that's a great idea. Do you need money?"

Kim shook her head. "No thanks. I'm OK."

I'm OK, she repeated silently. *I'm OK. OK.*

But she wasn't. Lately, these last few weeks, she'd been getting worse again. More and more often she dreaded again, and remembered, how right it felt just to let go and crawl back into the black hole and its comfort of hate and misery.

She mustn't, of course. She mustn't, for Jamie's sake. She mustn't, for her mother's sake. She mustn't, for her own sake. She mustn't, for so many sakes that she lost track far too often, but one day, she kept telling herself, one day she'd stop it once and for all, when the time was right, when no one's sake was at stake. And that, she knew, wasn't a wish, it was a fact. She just had to learn to be patient.

In the meantime she'd keep hiding behind the masks they all wanted her to wear because they couldn't stand to look at what she was without them. She had a collection of them by now, all the different smiles and frowns, the buffoon act with which she fooled her friends, the brave look her mother liked so much, the self-mocking one she liked the least, the I'm-busy-but-OK look when she was at wit's end, and, most important, the plain look, which was the hardest because there were no instructions for just plain.

Of course the masquerade simply confirmed what they all knew but couldn't or wouldn't admit: that no one could do anything for her, not Jamie, not her parents, not her teachers, certainly not Dr. Spencer. Even her friends could only let her down. The pills helped, but they changed nothing about the fact that she was alone.

"You have no idea how good you have it," her mother said, putting the cloth away.

Ah yes, there she went again with the same old story of how hard she'd had it herself growing up, how poor her family had been, how dysfunctional and screwed up.

"Mom, this is my life, not yours."

A car pulled up in the driveway. Kim put her empty bowl into the dishwasher and went to answer the door.

"Hi," she yelled as Jamie came loping up the pavement. "It's Jamie," she called out to her mother, who stood in the kitchen doorway.

"Why don't you ask him in?" her mother asked.

"There's no time," Kim reminded her, and ran upstairs.

She locked herself in the bathroom and fished for her toothbrush. She heard her mother ask Jamie whether he cared for a cup of coffee. What was it with her mother? Why couldn't she mind her own business? Why did she always have to get things so confused? First she went on about running late, now she was asking Jamie in for a coffee.

Kim caught her eyes in the mirror. They looked feverish. She could see pain in them and wondered whether her mother had picked up on it as well. She felt ugly this morning, her hair too brown, her face too round, her cheekbones too high, her lips too fleshy for too small a mouth. She had a reputation for being pretty. She once thought so herself, but not lately. Prettiness wasn't a matter of shape but of something else, something she no longer possessed and hadn't in a long time. Prettiness, too, was just a mask now.

"Kim! You'll be late!"

This time her mother was right. Kim put on lip gloss, gave her hair a quick brush, threw one more glance at her image already fleeing the mirror, and rushed downstairs.

"I like your mother," Jamie said, as they pulled out of the driveway.

She didn't feel like answering, but it came out anyway, half truth, half lie. "So do I."

Dr. Spencer had told her to concentrate on liking herself first. But that turned out to be easier said than done. No one, not even Jamie, had been able to convince her that there was anything to like. Most of the time she just hated herself. And didn't that give her the right to hate all the others as well, including her mother? Wasn't it part of her mother's role in this family problem her depression had become to allow herself to be hated so she, Kim, could take the pressure off herself?

She felt Jamie's eyes on her and turned to face him. "What?"

"You and your mother need to talk," he said.

"She doesn't want to because her own guilt is killing her."

"Well, it is tough, isn't it?"

She shrugged. "I don't see why. It was my choice, not hers."

For the record, the night had started off with one of the best

Sunday dinners they'd had in a long time. Not a single quarrel the previous two weeks, her mother relaxed and chatty as she served the roast, the twice-baked potatoes, the vegetables glazed with brown sugar. She'd even baked a pie. They'd watched TV after that, curled up on the couches and loungers as one happy family, and she herself thinking without one shred of regret that this was the way it would be like every Sunday evening if she wasn't around to spoil it.

She'd loved them more than ever that evening—her mother, who was really just very screwed up; her father, whose biggest fault was that he lacked assertiveness; her younger brother and sister, who were still too young not to be lovable. They might hate her for some time, but they could at least get on with their lives, and she could get on with whatever there was after death.

Then she was alone with her stockpile of pills. Even she wasn't sure what happened next, whether she laughed or cried or both. It seemed she felt everything at once and wanted it to last forever. She knew she'd made the right decision and all there was left to do was to get on with it. She hadn't counted on her little brother having a nightmare and coming into her room for a cuddle.

That was six months ago. Her mother still didn't want to talk about it. All she wanted was to know why. Of course, the correct though forbidden answer was, Why not? It summed up everything, the night, the evening that had led to it, all the empty years she remembered and those she didn't. "Haven't I loved you enough?" her mother wanted to know the first time they'd seen Dr. Spencer together. "Too much and too little," she'd replied, and that was as far as they ever got.

Jamie pulled into the next gas station. As she watched him fill up the car, she went once more over the talk on depression and suicide she'd agreed to give at her old high school. During the arrangements, Mr. Morris, the principal, had told her she was "one courageous young woman." Well, courage had absolutely nothing to do with any of it, more like a tangle of flaws that had turned them all, including her, into cowards.

She gave Jamie a wide smile as he got back behind the wheel and started the car.

"You know," she said, feeling as light as a feather. "*Why not?* may not be the ultimate answer either, but it will have to do. At least for now."

Jamie pulled into the street with a frown. Kim leaned back in her seat, repeating the mental exercise Dr. Spencer had prescribed. *I can do this. I can do this.*

A poster had started to appear downtown on power poles, on parking lot walls, on the community boards of corner stores.

Children Need Limits, it said.

Staring out of it was the face of a middle-aged man, balding, with friendly but firm eyes. He looked like a politician running for office, though no election of any kind was scheduled. Under his picture was the name of a meeting hall and a date.

Ned Gillis passed the poster stapled to one of the poles at the intersection of Duckworth and Prescott, turned, passed it a second time, turned again, and stopped.

The man was right, he thought. Children had no respect for their elders anymore. Young people were out of control. Too many parents didn't have enough time for themselves, let alone for their children. The world was a mess. Everyone had memories of better times, though the details were vague.

Children Need Limits.

Gillis reacted too late to the sound of the approaching car. Its front wheels hit the puddle at the bottom of the pole just as he prepared to jump. He was drenched from the waist down.

He felt the poster eyes burning into his back as he turned to curse the fleeing car.

You see? they said.

THE PHONE CALL

The snow was soft and grainy, like coarse sugar, and very fast. His skis glided like skates. Every now and then a dollop slipped off a branch and struck him as he passed.

Peter Drodge reached the edge of the airport. Dense fog hung over the runways. He fell into a skating stride, poling over his left leg, moving with shuffling fluency. A jet droned deep inside the whiteness beyond the fence, filling it with bored tension.

His cellphone rang. He stopped.

"Yes?"

"Bert?" a voice asked.

"No, this is Peter."

"I want to talk to Bert," the voice said.

"Sorry. You got the wrong number."

"No. You don't understand. I need to talk to Bert."

"Well, try Bert's number then. This is my number, and I'm not Bert."

There was no reply.

"Hello?"

A stifled sob.

"Hello?"

The line went dead. He shrugged and resumed skiing.

The droning of the jet became more insistent. He thought he detected an edge of impatience.

The phone rang again. The same voice asked for Bert.

"Who's calling?" he asked.

"It's me. John."

"Listen, John. I told you this isn't Bert's phone. It's mine. My name isn't Bert, it's Peter. I have no idea who this Bert of yours is. Are you sure you dialed the right number?"

Silence.

"John! Are you there?"

"I really need to talk to Bert."

"Well, I can't help you there." He didn't like the way that had come out. It occurred to him that John was in some kind of trouble. "Listen," he said, "are you OK?"

Another sob.

"John?"

"I'm not feeling too good," John said.

"What's the problem?"

"Are you sure you're not Bert?"

"Yes, I'm sure I'm not Bert. Who's Bert?"

"Man, you just don't understand."

The line went dead.

He imagined a teenager in his room, plugged into music, high on something and scared, the walls plastered with posters of punk rock bands and lyrics scribbled all over the place, most of them about how savagely beautiful and pointless life is, all one loud scream, and not even his own but something he'd cobbled together from the huge selection of screams being peddled as music these days. He'd struggled to find his own voice but didn't know where to look, so he'd gone looking for one that felt right, and now there was no end to the screaming in his room and in his head. He still thought it was his own pain he was hearing.

Peter thought of his own three children—Debbie, Danny, and Jake—and felt a stab in the pit of his stomach. None of them was anything more or less than the average package of fulfilled and unfulfilled hopes and promises. Wasn't that enough?

Linda, their mother, certainly thought so. But he wasn't so sure. Too many parents wasted their own and their children's time waiting to be proven right when they knew they'd been wrong all along. And even when the children did pull away from the precipice, as most of them did, it was their accomplishment, not that of their parents, waiting to be redeemed.

No, no, he corrected his thoughts. It wasn't the parents, it was the system. Never had it been harder to be young. Everybody knew that the challenge for the young was no longer making it to the other side, the side of the adults; their challenge was to survive the ghettos on their own side, the preteens, junior high, and high school.

Granted, Debbie had sailed through it all with consummate common sense, and Danny had done so-so. But Jake had gotten lost, started drifting, and hanging out, and drowning in loud and aimless anger. He'll be all right, Linda had kept saying because, despite all her protesting, Jake was her favourite. All right? How? It was a miracle any of them made it, locked up inside their teenage culture and kept there until the system decided they were ready to be released. For crying out loud, an entire arm of government called the Department of Education was assigned to keeping them locked up. Everything was done to institutionalize them inside their own confusion, and then, all of a sudden, they were expected to grow out of it?

Linda accused him of exaggerating as usually. But was he? The world was crawling with baby boomers who've been herding their children into the reservations of teen culture so they can claim the realm of youth all for themselves. Parents everywhere were acting younger than their own kids. No wonder teenagers were turning into a problem. What choice did they have but to play the game of unproductive dependents, a drain on family resources and a source of endless guilt for all concerned?

Hold on, Linda's voice reminded him. *Didn't Jake grow out of it? So he hung around for years doing too little, but didn't he go to trade school in the end, train as a welder, and end up making good money working in the Alberta oil patch?*

A high snowdrift cut across the trail and forced Peter to herring-bone his way over it. Halfway down the other side he lost his nerve and fell.

Shit!

It took what seemed like forever to extricate himself from the tangle of poles, skis, and his legs. He had a flashback to Linda standing in the front door as he put his skis in the car, telling him to be careful. He'd told her not to worry, he was well insured. She'd given him a cold look of disapproval and turned back into the house without waving goodbye.

A sharp regret tore through his gut. He pushed the redial button on his cellphone.

"Bert?" John answered eagerly.

"No, it's Peter."

"What the fuck do you want?"

"I just want to make sure you're OK."

"What the fuck?"

"Watch your language, boy! You called me. Remember?"

"I want to talk to Bert, not to a creep like you."

"Well, next time get the number straight. Right now I'm talking to you."

He heard him move, perhaps off his bed. A door opened. Someone hawked in a confined space and spat.

"You OK?"

"What do you care? Who the fuck are you?"

"Someone who cares." He regretted it as soon as he said it. It had just slipped out, as banalities do.

"Jesus!" John said, and the line went dead.

The droning inside the fog suddenly revved into a roar. The roar turned into a scream, a letting go of all restraint, and for a moment Peter thought the very air was going to come apart.

But it held, and as it did, the scream hardened into a tense, high-pitched chant of pure determination. Then it dissolved into rapidly fleeing motion.

His phone rang again. It startled him. He tried to ignore it, but it kept on ringing. He thought if John wanted to speak to him that badly perhaps it was worth another try.

It was Linda.

"I'm sorry, I don't mean to interrupt your skiing. But Doris called. She says it's urgent. Will you be much longer? Of course I can take a cab. I just thought I'd check."

There were at least two messages. The first, Linda really didn't want to take a cab; the second, that since she didn't get along all that well with her sister, she would much rather he came along.

"I've gone as far as I wanted to anyway," he lied. "I can be home in about an hour. How's that?"

He turned and headed back. The plane had left. The edge of the airport felt empty and deserted. He knew it was pointless, but he stopped one last time and redialed John's number. He let it ring a dozen times, then disconnected.

And then at last he heard the silence he'd come looking for between the sounds around him, the beating of his heart, the cawing of a crow a few treetops away, the complaining of a revved-up engine beyond the trees, the static rumble of moving traffic in the far distance. He closed his eyes and could have sworn he heard even the snow melting under his skis.

Everyone agreed that he was born against all good judgment. His father had been the wrong man, his mother too young. The circumstances had sucked. All his life he'd served as a reminder of how things can go off the rails.

Perhaps as a result of all that, he had limited common sense. He wasn't stupid or disabled in any way. He had a quick mind and quick hands and feet, wasn't a bad looker, was generally well liked both inside and outside his family. But he carried on him the mark of a defeat which wasn't his but that of his parents. It wasn't fair, but fairness had nothing to do with it.

The best advice he ever got was from Sarah.

"Fuck them!" she said.

"It's not that easy," he pointed out.

"Fuck them anyway!"

THE DREAM

For years, the *Betty D.* had been delivering fuel and freight to the dozen or so isolated communities on the south coast. Now she was up for sale. There had been talk that she was heading south to some place in the Caribbean.

Dave Dillon found Jimmy, her custodian, where he'd gone looking for him: in the ship's galley, about to pour himself tea.

"Any news?" he asked.

Jimmy shrugged. "Next m...m...month, th...th...they say."

"Mind if I hang out?"

"M...m...m...make yourself c...c...comfortable."

Jimmy poured Dave a cup, picked up a cloth and started wiping the table down. Dave watched him switch hands as easily as if he was playing them off against each other.

"What's that word again? Ambisomething?"

"Amb...b...b...bid...d...d...dextrous."

"You always been ambi-whatever?"

Jimmy shook his head. Dave reached for his cup, studying his own left hand as it performed the task.

"I don't know why I was such a stubborn son of a bitch about it myself," Dave said. "I mean, more like stupid when I think of it. I wasn't going to give in to them, not me. That left hand of mine meant everything to me, like it made me special. Someone should have told me that I could have had it both ways, like you. But no, they said there was only one way, and I told myself if it's not my way, well then, screw them. Did I ever tell you they were going to kill me because of it? My own folks?"

Of course he did, but some things need repeating. He knew Jimmy didn't mind, so he let the old grievance flow once more until there was nothing more to say.

Jimmy poured them more tea, then started to read the paper. The heat of the galley oozed into Dave. His eyes fought to stay open. His head kept dropping. The purr of the ship's generator set him afloat, and he went under.

Everybody has gathered on the meadow in Bowring Park, all the employees of Barry Steamships Ltd., including the founder of the company, old Noah Barry himself. A train announces itself with a blow of its whistle as it comes clanging up the Waterford Valley.

Promises. Promises. Promises.

Bella, Noah Barry's great-granddaughter with the golden curls, grabs Jimmy by the hand and drags him toward the fence by the rail tracks. Everybody stops what they're doing and watch as the train makes it around the turn and clatters on in that chugging doomed way it has. Silence falls over the crowd, a hush of awe, pleasure, regret, anger, and betrayal. A few people clap and cheer. Then the blankets come out and spill baskets that burst into picnics.

Dave is in the midst of it all, entertaining and delighting the party by taking big leaps that vault him high into the air. And his father is there, holding a serious discussion with Toby, Noah Barry's oldest son. For once no one treats him like the loser he is. He waves, and Dave comes down from his last leap. They walk away from the crowd.

"I loved you," his father says. He's wearing a cod face with big, lidless eyes, his breath rasping over his gills. Before he speaks again, his face changes into that of a beaver, grave and helpless.

"You were my firstborn, if I count out Lilly, who gave us nothing but trouble from day one until she died in her crib howling and screaming. She was always screaming, like her mother. But you, you were a gem until we discovered that you were one of those lefties. It wasn't your fault, it wasn't, and I'm sorry now we gave you such a hard time."

A tear rolls down his cheek, and then another, and another. And then he's gone. A thick fog has come up. Dave hears the splash of the oars and Uncle Mose's deep voice striking up the psalm.

"Ask of me, and I shall give thee the heathen for thine inheritance, and the uttermost parts of the earth for thy possession. Thou shalt break them with a rod of iron. Thou shalt dash them in pieces like a potter's vessel."

Uncle Mose stands at the stern of the punt, full of his ugly holier-than-thou self. He's parting the fog with outstretched arms as if it was the Red Sea. Aunt Agnes cowers at his feet, her big flesh all over the place, that swollen body of hers which knows every one of Uncle Mose's sins, those huge childless breasts, and those thighs which spread over the tawt on which she sits like two monster loaves of rising bread.

"Keep that devil's hand out of my sight," thunders Uncle Mose.

"Don't," Aunt Agnes whines. "Come here, boy, I'm going to sprinkle some holy water on it."

Dave hides his left hand behind his back.

"Now look what you've done," Uncle Mose screeches. Aunt Agnes tries to reach out, but her arms are too short and too fat.

"I know," she says to Dave, pleading. "I've told everybody you're the devil's spawn because your father was a bad man. He killed your mother, my baby sister, by breaking her heart. I'm not lying to you, so give me your hand."

Dave keeps his eyes on Uncle Mose. There's murder in that man's eyes again, but he can't get around Aunt Agnes, who whimpers, "It's not right, Mo. It's not right."

"What are you talking about? You saw him yourself, crossing himself with his left hand. The little fucker did it on purpose."

Aunt Agnes opens her mouth. Her fat lips move and white bubbles come streaming out like little bits of empty prayer.

"You bitch!" Uncle Mose sings out as if starting another psalm. Aunt Agnes has tipped over and lies in the bottom of the punt like a beetle on its back, her eyes rolling, more bubbles pouring from her lips. Dave raises the cursed hand and holds it out like a weapon. It's a claw now, black and shrivelled, and he can feel its hunger for power. But he can't remember the password. All he can think of are the words to Hail Mary, and they're no good.

Aunt Agnes floats off among her bubbles and starts to turn white. Uncle Mose sits on the tawt now, his arms hanging over the oars. He looks tired and shakes his head.

"I destroyed them with water. I destroyed them with fire. I set them warring on each other. I sent them plagues of every description. Nothing's worked. I will humble them with love, and they will serve their time out in guilt."

Dave felt something shake him by the arm. He opened his eyes.

"I'm m...m...m...making some supper. You s...s...staying?"

"How long have I been asleep?"

"Ever s...s...s...since you g...g...g...got here."

Jimmy dropped a plate in front of him. In no time at all there were two fried eggs on it, sunny side up, beans, and four strips of crispy bacon. A bottle of ketchup appeared. Slabs of white bread and a tub of margarine followed.

"You wan...n...n...a say the b...b...blessing?"

"Hell, no," Dave said, reaching for his fork and knife. "You know what? I did go to see Aunt Agnes a couple of months ago, just like you said I should. She's not all there anymore. She thinks I'm the son she never had."

He put his fork and knife down again and looked up, struggling.

"I told her."

"Y...y...y...you told her w...w...what?"

"I told her what really happened. You know, I just wanted to put an end to it, like make up after all the years. So I'd offered to help Uncle Mo fix his roof on account of his weakness due to his heart condition. I thought we were getting along just fine up there on the roof, but he said something about me using my left hand to drive the nails, and it all came up again. I was going to throw him off, I swear I was going to. But he just laughed at me and jumped himself. Just like that. Broke his neck. I don't know if Aunt Agnes understood when I told her. She just smiled like it was the biggest joke in the world."

Jimmy nodded quietly, thinking it over. Dave nodded back, picked up his fork and knife again, and started to eat.

They call themselves children of the Book, and this book, they claim, was given to them by me.

Well, I gave them nothing of the sort. They gave it to themselves. I'm not nearly the meddler they would have me be.

GOD LOVES YOU

The winter had been unusually cold and dry. Now, as the days were getting longer, leaves were rattling up and down the street like so much unfinished business. Joel glanced back at the warm glow of light coming from the window of the corner store he'd just left, hunched into his parka, and pushed his way into the dark no man's land where March chases November.

It was snowing. He ducked through the hole in the chain-link fence, crossed the empty playground, and entered the lane that ran into the street leading to his apartment building. A blow and then the sound of wood rending and splintering caught his ear. It came from inside the swirling darkness of Bob Maher's backyard.

Another blow followed and another.

"Bob?" he called.

The blows stopped.

"Bob! It's me! Joel."

The wind hissed and thumped around the yard like something gone berserk in a cage. Bob materialized with a scowl on his face, but he lit up as he came within speaking range.

"God loves you," he said.

Joel knew the answer was *God loves you too*.

"Well, I wouldn't know," Joel said. "He's never told me so himself."

"You're not listening," Bob replied.

A squall heavy with snow slammed into them, rattled some loose boards, and whooshed off with the reply that had been on the tip of Joel's tongue. Listening to what? To your heart, his neighbour Suzanne would have said. Heart is for suckers, he would have corrected her. Who taught you to be so tough? she might have corrected him back.

Another gust nearly swept him off his feet. Bob staggered as well and reached for the fence to steady himself. He seemed so helpless with that fever in his eyes.

"How are things coming?" Joel asked.

"I received the final instructions two nights ago," Bob said, moving closer and lowering his voice. "I can't talk about it, but The Twelve are ready. Everything's arranged now. Everything."

Yes, everything was arranged. Not by God though, but by whatever it was that had made itself at home in Bob's head. And it was clearly up to no good again.

"Look, I've got to go," Joel said holding up the shopping bag with the loaf of bread and the block of cheese he'd bought at the store.

"God loves you." Bob nodded and turned back into his yard.

God loves you. It kept going through Joel's mind as he entered the lobby of the apartment building. What did God really know about love? So he took a few trips to earth every now and then, lived out a few holy lives that started religions here and there and the bloodshed that came with them. Did he have the slightest idea what was really going on, what Bob was up to in his backyard, what anyone was up to, for that matter?

And what God anyway? The one of Chapter I, who loves only one tribe and beats up on all the others? The one of Chapter II, who lives in a temple run by butchers and money-changers? The one of Chapter III, who sides with the enemy? The one of Chapter IV, who comes down to earth dressed up as his own son and has himself slaughtered so his blood can be on everybody's hands? Or the one of the chapter still in progress, who could be anything anywhere depending on who told the story? And now it seemed God was getting ready to pull the plug again, and he'd given Bob detailed instructions for turning his shed into the portal for the chosen, a main chamber for The Twelve, side chambers for other increasingly larger groups which would start arriving once The Twelve were gathered.

And who were The Twelve?

Only they knew.

But what guided them?

God, of course.

How, with a star?

Who knows. God had many ways of showing the way.

And the others?

Oh, they'll know, but they have to learn to open their hearts first.

Still, even Bob admitted there was a problem. Not one local engineer had shown an interest in God's demand for the construction of an underground city below the Southside Hills. Officials at city hall had given the idea nothing but cold shoulders. So had the folks at the Board of Trade. And the few local churchmen known to be preaching the coming days of the end had dismissed the mission as if it were unwelcome competition.

Lately Bob had been wondering himself: what if it wasn't God who was speaking to him? What if it was the Enemy, who was second only to God in cleverness and power? So he'd gotten down on his knees and prayed, and he still wasn't absolutely sure, and it tormented him day and night.

Joel knocked on Suzanne's door across the hall from his own apartment. It was Suzanne who'd introduced him to Bob in the first place. He wanted to tell her that the fever in Bob's eyes was starting to worry him. Suzanne must have been out because she didn't answer.

Back in his own place, he made himself a grilled cheese sandwich, which he washed down with a beer. He was annoyed with Suzanne for not being in. He turned on the TV but wasn't interested in the game shows and sitcoms. He picked up a book but put it down before he'd read one line. He walked to the window and watched snowflakes slam into the glass, melt, and run down as if in defeat. Bob's greeting kept coming into his mind like a tune that wouldn't go away. *God loves you. God loves you. God loves you.* He felt restless, a stranger in his own apartment. He put the bottle away, the plate in the sink, and dressed to go back outside. He hated the idea of braving the storm again but felt he owed Bob another conversation.

Bob's yard lay under the silence of rapidly accumulating snow. A wedge of light was falling across the ground from the half-open door of the shed. Joel called. There was no answer. He called again, pushed the gate open, crossed the yard, and entered the shed.

The stench of emptied bowels hit him first. Then his eyes found the dangling feet and travelled up the legs to the arms hanging straight down, the neck twisted by the cord tied to a rafter, the protruding tongue and bulging eyes, the brutal blue that had engorged Bob's face.

Joel's first thought was how long had it taken for Bob's spirit to make its escape from this hideous carcass; his second, how he would tell Suzanne. And then he wondered who, if anyone, would write Bob's obituary. He imagined it opening with *I accuse*. For Suzanne's sake he settled on *Survived and lovingly remembered by God*.

A prayer

*You, who are all around,
let us get you right.
Your chaos be our order,
your necessities our design
within as well as without.*

*Let us live on what we must
and free us from guilt
as we would free others from it,
and lead us not into mirrors
but deliver us from ourselves.*

*For you are it
for better and for worse.*

Amen

TO WHOM IT MAY CONCERN

I hear it every Sunday coming from the temples and churches they keep building for me, and it's always the same question: How much do I love them?

I never have to answer, because they insist that I love them infinitely. What else, they reason, could explain and excuse their hardships, their dark winters, the few months of sunshine in late summer and fall, the stiff-necked land and sea from which they're trying to eke a living.

If I were to answer, it would be with another question: What do they really know about me?

I am what I am. In me every possibility is inevitable, every choice is a destiny. This is the simple fact over which humans have been making far too much mystifying fuss. Consider what they call my divine purpose. There's no such thing because I already am everything I ever was and ever will be. They, on the other hand, can only see themselves coming and going, and they need purpose to make sense of that.

Are they dear to my heart? No more and no less than they're dear to their own hearts.

So let's talk about love. Yes, I loved Adam inasmuch as he loved me. He was the first of them, if you count out Lilith, who got lost in the shuffle. Adam was a gem. What happened wasn't his fault, nor was it Eve's. The two had no way of knowing, because the whole thing was between me and my creation and therefore myself. They got caught in the middle, but so does everything. If I had to defend myself, I'd simply say that I didn't see it coming because it already existed long before it happened.

The love between Adam and me grew after he chose death and wasn't going to be around forever, at least in his own experience. Poor Adam! How he misunderstood his fall from grace. And what damage guilt can do. It made him and his descendants form the idea of sin, and that's turned them into churlish and ungrateful creatures.

They keep insisting that I had it all planned. What they don't understand is that I simply am the plan. Whether I make their hardships and deliverances happen or whether they just happen by themselves, it's all one and the same. I have no agenda other than myself, and they still don't understand the full implications of that.

They would have my greatest gift to them be love. Looking at it from their perspective, I agree, though technically it was they who brought love into play as they did so many other things. It's one of their flaws, perhaps the greatest, that they see their imperfections as an evil which must be redeemed. Love, I'd have them know—but they're quite aware of it themselves by now—destroys as much as it redeems.

Adam and Eve preferred Abel and his animals over Cain and his crops. I can't say that I preferred either. Still, Adam asked me to favour Abel's sacrifices and felt I owed him that much. Perhaps I was playing with the smoke of Cain's fire to please Adam, though more likely it was just a windy day that came with the first chill of envy and hate.

Cain blamed the murder on me, so he learned to hate me, and through this hate he started to view me more and more like himself. I understood then that I'd turned the table on myself. I'd created humans in my own image; now they were creating me in theirs. Watching them is like looking into a mirror that distorts everything I am.

And let's get another thing straight: I had nothing to do with the flood they so neatly concocted into some kind of contract between them and me. They brought it upon themselves with the way they treated and denuded the land. I didn't have to tell Noah anything. He saw it coming all by himself.

It was such a dreary, clammy day when their ark finally struck land. No one on board wanted to make the first move because the place was covered in mud, and mud was not what they'd hoped for. It was Ham—he reminded me of Cain—who finally sloshed his way to the outcrop on which they built a small altar and sacrificed one of the sheep they'd brought with them.

Yes, I blessed Noah and told him in so many of his own words to be fruitful and multiply and replenish the earth. I did not say that fear and dread should be upon everything else after that. I remember what a pitiful pile of rocks their altar was, and that they had trouble lighting the damp straw and were just about to give up when the sun broke through the still swollen clouds and cast a rainbow. There were so many rainbows in those days, but this one came along just at the right time. I understand they needed a sign and preferred a rainbow over the foul smoke of their sacrifice, but their claim that it was my signature under a pact they expected to strike with me is entirely their fiction. If I let them believe that all living creatures were delivered into their hands, I meant them to include themselves, and I intended it as a caution, not as an invitation to pillage.

And I did not go out of my way to confuse their language when they built that tower in Babel. They put it up because they hoped it would unite them. They meant it to be a lasting declaration of the belief that they were all born equal. But the more they worked on it, the more it pushed them apart. I had nothing to do with it, absolutely nothing. Only later, much later, when their memories started to fail them, did they blame the whole thing on me. Hence the self-serving story of how they challenged me, how I pushed back and punished them for their arrogance. Once again they did it to themselves. The structure was so complex—it had so many levels, so many different layers of command from its construction to the running of it— one single language was simply not going to work.

They've never been good at standing up for themselves, at answering directly for their actions. They make up stories instead. The story of how they contracted sin is not their oldest, yet by the way they keep telling it, they'd have themselves believe that it is. Neither is sin their oldest excuse, but it's been their most widely used. Perhaps back then they saw sin and the guilt that fans it as a means to achieve humility. From what I've observed, it's had the opposite effect. There's pride, not humility, in their relentless demand to be judged.

Contrary to everything humans have said and written, I've not made a special project of them, even where conditions are harsh and the thought of being favoured or singled out might help ease their struggles. But I do think about them, because thinking is what they brought to the table. I'm entertained by it, elated, saddened, conflicted, frustrated, and countless other reactions. At times it terrifies me, because nothing plumbs the improbable and impossible like human thought. And deep inside this mirror, which even I fear, lies the truth that they're right: it is all my doing.

The short prayer

Hey, you, wherever you are,
hallowed be thy name, whatever it is,
thy kingdom come because our kingdoms don't work,
thy will be done despite all the evidence to the
>*contrary,*
up your way, where there's no argument,
and down here, where too many don't care.

Amen

P.S. DEI

I ask myself sometimes—which, in my case, is forever—how humans came along in the first place. It's not as if the creation I've become needs them. It would be better off without them. It's been suggested that I was lonely. There have been many other explanations. Here is mine.

The only way I can figure myself out is by manifestation, and so I've manifested myself, from my first step out of chaos to the complexities of life upon which I stumbled quite by predictable chance. I knew right away there was something about life which was different from everything else I've become. I never cease to be surprised by its accommodations and absurdities, to wonder at its obsession with itself, to be amused by how it continues to re-invent itself. In life I feel myself moving both closer and further away from myself. I've recognized it as my own reflection, and I never tire of staring back into it.

And then came humans. They like to stare at themselves as well. They have that from me. Sometimes I worry about this vanity, about what it's doing to them and to me. But no, there was no special creation, just another manifestation of myself in a particular kind of image—not strictly my own, but something that I craved.

Sometimes I do get tired of this aspect of myself, but I can't control it. Humans have become my voice. If only they could hear themselves as I hear them.

DINNER AT THE KELLANDS

It was a small crowd as our host, Don Kelland, had promised. Mary, his adventurous wife, served a chicken dish with Creole colours and flavours. She said she had modified it to suit our temperate palates. If she had misjudged us, we were welcome to add the hot sauce she had placed in small dishes around the table.

There was no need to add sauce to the food, the conversation was spicy enough. We opened with the weather, moved on to the latest gossip, then discussed the growing ethnic diversity of our city and the popular perception that every male who prays to Allah is a potential terrorist and any female who veils her face a victim. Someone commented that religion is the source of all conflict, someone else that religion has to be seen not as the source but as a particularly efficient—perhaps too efficient—conductor of conflict. The mating rituals of certain spiders came up, which led us to the topic of predation and human behaviour, which made us pause.

We served ourselves more chicken and rice and poured more wine.

"You know, coming back to religion," Kelland said. "You have to ask yourself what is it really all about. I suppose you have to grow up inside a particular religion to appreciate what it has to offer, how it helps people make sense of their particular world and at what price, because there's always a price. All I know is that, besides its fixation on love, which has its merits, Christianity is of questionable usefulness. And I think the reason is that it ignores its true roots."

We humoured him by looking puzzled.

"Let me explain," he continued. "According to Christian tradition, there are two places of sacred territory in this otherwise profane and hostile universe. One is the central isle of Heaven, where God resides. The other is the individual soul dropped into the troublesome acre that is life on earth with one mission and one mission only: to find its way back to Heaven. It's a quest against enormous odds, and failure, as we all know, means eternal damnation, a particularly nasty form of death.

"Now I ask you, where have you heard this before, this story of millions born to swarm and wiggle and bump their way toward the great promise? If I can ask you to put aside all the taboos and other gimmicks of prejudice that have been stacked against reproduction, if you can step past the agreed-upon indecency of it, the moaning and groaning and sweating and animal-like surrender to lust and raw instinct, then I think the picture is perfectly clear. The Christian world view is the story of the sperm and its mission to unite with the egg.

"And I ask you, what else can we expect from a religion cobbled together by men? It's men who made up the stories we've lived with for thousands of years, men who told and retold them in their temples and bible schools, men who determined what's allowed and what isn't and construed their own basic role in nature to be the main plot for the universe.

"And so we've ended up with a religion whose obsession with such things as predestination and grace amounts to little more than grim admissions that freedom of choice and self-determination are vanities by which sperm perish in the millions at every rush for salvation."

He gave us a brief moment to reflect as we looked at him, speechless, then he continued.

"Now ask yourself, what would our religious beliefs be if we saw them through the female perspective, which is that of the egg, if we agreed that our role is not to escape into another world but to be completed in this one? I'm not saying it would be all sunshine and peaches, but the whole notion of swarming out in order to find would be replaced by staying put in order to receive. And when your goal is to receive, is it not in your own interest to see the world around you as your ally rather than as your enemy? And if the world is your ally, there's no need for a devil in the works. Everything would be divine, not just zillions of scattered bits down here and one big and impossibly far-away chunk up there. Everything would be awash with sacredness. The whole thing would be one blessed event. And perhaps then we would stop blowing each other up in the name of God."

Mary smiled discreetly but triumphantly. One of the two couples at the table had frozen into embarrassed silence. The other, a social planner with the city and her husband, a recently graduated nurse practitioner, rose to the occasion with a well-meaning but painfully inane rehash of how women have been shortchanged by men over the ages. I, for my part, wondered whether Kelland was simply afraid that he was not going to make it to Heaven himself.

―――――――――――

If she had the powers of creation, if it was her will that was to be done, it would be a very orderly world.

Yes, there would be all kinds of pleasures, but surprise would not be among them. A world ruled by her would be pitilessly structured for all the right reasons. No one would fail to signal at the appropriate time. People would stand in line as they're supposed to. There would be no unexpected jumps in oil and gas prices. There would be no junk mail and spam. Nothing would ever break down except the odd vacuum cleaner, because she had a knack for fixing things like that.

There would be no disease, and if push came to shove, death would be banned as well. That is, if her will were to be done.

―――――――――――

UNFINISHED BUSINESS

Claire holds something in her hands as she looks out the window. I think it's the locket I bought for her at the garage sale last week, the one with the photograph she says reminds her so much of her great-grandmother whom she never met but should have because they have so much in common (she has yet to explain what).

"Just look at all the leaves blowing about," she says.

I'm seated on the couch with the *Collected Works of Oscar Wilde* on my lap. I stay put because I know Claire's just talking. That gets me thinking that there have been altogether too many words between us. The longer we know each other and the better we know the patterns, the more random we seem to become. And that, too, feels like a pattern.

I picture those leaves. I've seen them a hundred times and more, blowing up and down our street.

"The window?" I ask. "Who was it that said you have to smash it if you want to experience things instead of just looking at them?"

Claire turns and gives me a long searching look. She's studying me from a great distance and making no attempt to hide it. I see now that it's not the locket she's playing with; it's the cluster of amethyst crystals we keep on the windowsill.

"Mallarme," she says. "Stephane Mallarme. You once called him a coward. Remember?"

"Ah, yes. Mallarme. He liked to pontificate."

"So do you."

Claire turns back to the window. She lays the crystals on the sill with great tenderness as if putting down something newborn. She resumes her watch. What's she looking for? A sign? After all these years?

Today's one of those days when I don't know what to do with myself. Something draws me with a deep ache but I don't know what, and even if I did know, I'm not sure I could respond to it. So I remain sitting on the couch, not even reading the book on my lap, just listening to the faint whisper of my longing.

Claire doesn't understand this mood in me. Maybe she doesn't want to. I've tried to explain it so many times, and she always reacts as if she's caught me once again putting more distance between us.

She speaks. "I was thinking this morning that it's time to get new pillows."

I picture two new pillows lying side by side on our bed. Two solitudes. I have no colours in mind for them, no patterns, no texture, just generic shapes like old dogmas no one questions anymore.

There! I've done it. I've put the book down and pushed myself off the couch. Now I'm walking into the bedroom for absolutely no other reason than that it was the first place that came not so much to my mind but to my body. The bed is still unmade.

"I think you're right," I call out. "We do need new pillows. I don't know how we've survived with these for so long."

It comforts me that I can't tell what she's laughing at, my sarcasm or something she sees through the window.

"We could go tomorrow," I add. "Make an afternoon of it."

"While we're at it, we could also look for curtains," Claire replies from the kitchen. "The blinds get so dusty. Can we do that?"

I'm tempted to remind her that we have unfinished business to take care of first: the sheets we forgot to buy the last time we went shopping.

I go to join her in the kitchen.

"We need a new water filter," she announces as I enter.

She's standing by the sink, turning the tap with one hand while holding a glass in the other. The light on the filter is flashing red.

I explain it's just a warning. As long as the filter's flashing, it's still working.

"I know. That's why we need a new filter."

"Yes, but you can still drink the water in the meantime."

She smiles.

I return to the living room, sit back on the couch, pick up the *Collected Works* again, and start reading *The Happy Prince*.

Claire has followed me and resumed her place at the window.

I'm thinking we need a new story. We've been stuck, she and I, in the same story for too long, so long I don't even know if there's still a plot, if in fact there ever was one.

"What do you think we would find out there if we did smash the window?"

"If I remember correctly, Mallarme was talking about poems, not relationships."

"Well, he was a symbolist."

"Your point?"

"We could smash it together."

Claire remains silent, but I can see her body tighten. This is my cue to get up, walk up to her, and undo whatever I've set in motion with a simple hug. But I stay on the couch, the *Collected Works* feeling absurdly heavy in my hands.

Claire seems far away now and lost.

"We should go for a walk," I force myself to suggest.

She starts, then sighs the way she did when we came home and realized we'd forgotten the sheets.

"Yes, we should."

I feel foolishly forgiven.

She was in the bathroom applying makeup when he walked in. He seemed quite unaware of her as he dropped his pajamas, moved toward the shower stall, turned on the water and tested it.

Like a specimen in a zoo, *she thought.* Powerful, healthy, well-kept, and completely unaware.

He stepped into the stall, closed the glass door, and started to whistle. Every now and then his whistling turned hoarse and broke. Then she pictured him licking his lips.

He's slipping away, *she thought,* and one day he'll turn around and blame it all on me. He'll say I changed him into an animal, the way the witch Circe did with the men foolish enough to put foot on her island.

That night, for the first time, he didn't come home.

"You've changed," *he said, as they sat down for a subdued supper the following evening.*

"So have you," *she replied.*

"No, I have not," *he protested, and she knew he was right.*

THE ANNOUNCEMENT

It's pouring rain. Even through the closed windows we can hear water splashing all around us. He's wearing his black housecoat. It hasn't been brushed in a while and is covered with lint. I don't know how and where in the house he picks it up, this white bloom of dust and other domestic particles which thrive on his housecoat. It's never on any of my clothes.

He walks across the living room and opens the window. The drumming of the rain rushes in like a call to reality. He stands there for a while as if inhaling it. Then he turns, his eyes crossing the floor until they find me.

"I need to move on," he announces.

I say nothing.

"It's my nature," he insists.

I'm thinking the racket coming in through the window proves him right. Nothing out there is safe. Nothing.

I need to focus him. He wants to tell me something but doesn't know how to and thinks he can get away by running.

"What's that supposed to mean?" I ask.

"It's not supposed to mean anything," he replies. "It's just the way it is."

He sounds irritated, backed into a corner. I know at that rate I won't have his attention much longer.

"And what?" I demand. "You just move on, and that's it?"

He shrugs. "I never promised anything. You should have known."

I wonder whether it would make any difference if I told him that I did know. I've known ever since we went to Europe this past summer. He proved that I was a total stranger by acting as if Europe belonged exclusively to him. On the whole trip he treated me like a travel companion who comes with the ticket. By the time we'd been through London, Cologne, Reims, Chartres (we avoided Paris), Tours, and Poitiers, we'd seen more cathedrals, more castles and fortresses than I could keep track of. They were his true home, he kept explaining as he dragged me from one to the other.

I finally raised the question on our flight back to St. John's. Home. Didn't he grow up in Twillingate, where the biggest structure was not a church or a fortress but the hockey rink and possibly one of the icebergs that come calling every late spring and early summer?

He replied it was obvious I made no effort to understand.

For God's sake, I exclaimed. What was there to understand?

Everything, he said.

That sounded more like nothing, I shot back.

He responded by looking wounded.

Cathedrals, castles, fortresses, I persisted. Why not graveyards, while we were at it? And that's what he considered his home? He replied, too smugly, I thought, that I was deliberately ignoring the full picture.

I still see him silhouetted against the porthole window of the plane, a cotton-candy sea of clouds in the distance below. Nothing matters, he said after a long pause, but some things hurt forever.

There was a time when that would have been my cue to back off and, by some unspoken agreement, allow him to take me once again to that other place he considered to be exclusively his: our bed, where he would be forgiven all over. On that day, the day of our return from Europe, I knew the time for forgiveness had passed.

And now the living room window frames him like an escape hatch disguised as our neighbourhood with its friendly houses and driveways across the street, the lawns trimmed just right, the sky behind it all like an undercoat of wet but harmless grey.

"You know," he says after another long silence, "I could contend that such and such doesn't matter, and you could counter that it does, and we could both be right. But when you hurt, there's no point in someone else telling you that you don't."

"So you're hurting?"

"Maybe," he says, and I can hear his voice tremble.

"Why don't we talk about it?"

"There's too much hurt everywhere," he replies.

I understand. He wants me to let him off the hook by feeling sorry, not for him but for the world. I'm tempted to ask him, so what have I been then, a stretch of desert he just happened to cross? Obviously not one of his castles. And I realize I've fallen into his trap and set him free.

"We men are born that way," he says, as if he's read my mind. "Born in solitude and destined to die in solitude. We're nomads."

Why can't he just come out with what's really bothering him? Is he bored? Is something missing? Is it the sex? The way I butter the toast, clean the dishes, make the bed? Is it my crazy family, which thinks the world of him?

"What is it then?" I ask. "After all, this is about both of us, not just you, and I have a right to know."

"What's the point of knowing?" he counters.

And I get it. He's telling me the decision isn't his and never was. It's mine. But I have no stomach for it. None whatsoever.

He moves suddenly and closes the window. I can tell by his abrupt manner that he thinks he's made the decision all by himself, and I feel cheated.

He turns and disappears in the bathroom without closing the door. I listen as he flushes the toilet, runs the tap, brushes his teeth, crosses the hallway, takes off his clothes, gets into bed, as if it was all part of closing the window.

There was a time when she didn't even know that she had a heart unless she made it work enough to set it pounding. These days it was always there, an ailing patient bedridden in the dark hollow of her chest, feverish, petulant, complaining. Dr. Lynch had demonstrated what he considered the problem with the help of a plastic model. A pump, he'd explained. A pump with slightly worn valves, but nothing tender loving care from her and a prescription from him couldn't handle. And he'd laughed the way parents do when they tell white lies.

"It's because he doesn't care," her friend Julia said. "These doctors—they think they can treat your heart like a pump. Valves and chambers! What do they really know about hearts? It was Bob who broke your heart 30 years ago, that's what. And you think Lynch can fix that with his pills?"

STELLA

There were days when she felt it, oh so faintly, so deep inside her bones, so far beyond reach that even the slightest attempt to focus on it scattered it like a wisp. Only a few times had it assumed enough shape for her to recognize a house, a picket fence, lace curtains, two presences in a room.

She'd felt it again this morning, standing by the stove. Something had stilled her—she had no idea what—the time-grinding cogs of the kitchen clock perhaps, and there they were, the fence, the house, the two shadows. This time she sensed a coziness of furniture, doily on table, kettle on stove, photographs on wall. She'd closed her eyes and created a tension between them which held all of it just long enough to hear a voice call her name. Then a wave of nausea had washed over her. Her heart had skipped several beats, and then it ached.

She'd dragged herself into the living room and lain down on

the couch and closed her eyes.

She's running through the field again. Oh, the joy! So much life, and so much joy! So much of her racing ahead, far too much of her holding her back, her heart wide open, and everything coming and going. Oh, so much joy, and so much love!

The schooner Gladys II *sits tied up at the wharf. A small crowd watches as the crew unloads the vessel with the help of a few men who've come down from their fishing stages. Stella has reached the line of backs and is pushing to get through, to get inescapably close, to smell the ship and its arrival, to know there are only a few familiar details left, the pattern of the rigging, the parallels of the planking, the cargo tumble of bales and barrels, and there they'll be, her father's arms closing around her.*

A hand stops her instead. She turns and stares into the face of Sam Brushett, the skipper of the Gladys II. *His hand perches on her shoulder like a bird's claw. His eyes are like hammers.*

"Come with me," he says.

She stays behind him as they walk back toward the village. Brushett is a short man, but he's used to giving orders and just as used to having them followed. His back draws her with its silence. She stares at the hand that clawed her shoulder. It has the look of a well-used tool, a blind and ruthless servant. She senses danger. He doesn't knock when they arrive at her house. He opens the door as if taking possession, walks in without calling out. She turns to catch a glimpse of her father coming up from the harbour, waving, his sailor's bag slung over one shoulder, but the path is empty.

She follows Brushett into the living room. It unsettles her to realize how much of it she's never noticed before, the naked walls behind the furniture, the spareness of the unfilled corners, the grim something on the floor she recognizes as her father's dufflebag. Her mother sits on the old daybed and looks blankly across the room, her hands in her lap. Stella has never seen so much emptiness in her face. Aunt Mary stands by the window looking out, her shawl drawn tightly around her shoulders as if to keep out a chill.

"Mom?" Stella says, turning to her mother. But her mother doesn't reply. Stella floods with panic. She looks for Brushett and sees him standing by the door to the hallway, the outsider now, awkward and diminished by something he knows he can't tell. He shakes his head instead.

Her brother Ben bursts into the room. "Dad!" he wails. Aunt Mary quietly crosses the room and wraps her arms around him.

The phone shrilled. Stella didn't want to answer it, but it kept on ringing, with each ring louder than the one before. She rose slowly, hoping it would stop before she got to it.

"Mom, are you OK?"

It was Alma, calling from Toronto.

"Why shouldn't I be?" Stella replied.

"You took so long to answer."

"Well, my dear, you kept it ringing long enough."

Stella knew that Alma never called just to enquire how she was. This was no exception. Alma asked whether she could come down for a week, a business opportunity, she didn't say what kind, but she couldn't afford a hotel, so could she stay at the house? Stella knew she was making a mistake but replied that she saw no reason why not.

"Thanks, Mom," Alma said. "Gotta go now. Love you." And she hung up.

Alma took after Bob, her father. She'd moved to Toronto because she was convinced that St. John's was too small for her. Yet her job as special assistant to some wheeler-dealer immigrant businessman wasn't even close to what she could have had down here with her secretarial skills and her smarts—a good job with the telephone company, a bank, even the government. But there was no point talking to her. Like her father she had no patience, she wanted to get rich, and she was willing to try her hand at any money-making scheme as long as it wasn't too illegal. Yet she could also be so thankful. Her brother, Brian, insisted it was all just a big act, but Stella knew that thankfulness from long before her daughter became so consumed with money. Maybe Brian didn't remember it because he was still too young, or he didn't want to remember because it meant his sister got off the hook again. Alma was innocent then, and some of that remained.

Stella made herself a cup of tea and sat down at the kitchen table. The window was open, allowing the stir of traffic from the neighbourhood to enter, the harbour rumble from downtown, the wail of the foghorn from the Narrows. She sipped her tea, sat very still, closed her eyes again and waited for the memories to come flooding back.

They live like eagles now. The house Brushett has built for them perches on Myles Rock high above every other roof and chimney in the village. Pieces of the bay squat across the front windows. Most times the water is leaden grey, but every now and then it turns to pure silver. The men down on the stages joke that should the fishery ever fail, they can just scoop their fortune off the water.

A boat rounds the headland, slices across a stretch of silver, swings into the tiny harbour, and ties up to the wharf. The band from Bay L'Argent has arrived, an accordion player, two fiddlers, and their hangers-on, hungry and thirsty and faceless as mummers. Brushett goes to get the rum. In the kitchen, Aunt Mary directs the neighbours' wives who've come to help assemble the wedding feast that's taking shape among bowls, platters, and pie pans, things rising and settling and waiting for their turn, cans opened, bottles uncorked, jars unlidded, and everywhere white drifts of flour. A litter of ale barrels huddles by the door. Six bottles of red wine from St. Pierre stand at attention on a side table.

And then the guests arrive—the women a gaggle of gossip, relaxed and driven by instinct straight into the kitchen; the men buttoned up and awkward, standing on some uptight ceremony they try to pass off as manliness, that rough look with hands dug into pockets for a reassuring clench of nothing. And there, sometimes on the edge of it all, sometimes right in the midst of it, is Uncle Walsh, sad and drunk and going on about what everybody has agreed not to mention: the man lost in the storm nine months earlier. Brushett never had a better first mate, and now he has his woman.

"Don't," Stella begs. Uncle Walsh keeps going until there's

enough booze in him to take him out.

For once Brushett has opened his purse wide. Food and drink pour from the kitchen like lava from a volcano. Stella watches him closely from where she sits next to the lump that only a short while before was Uncle Walsh. This, she says to the lump, is buying the gnome a night of everything that doesn't belong to him. Oh yes, she's figured it all out. How the Dwarf caught sight of Beauty and fell in greed with her sorrow. There she lay in the glass coffin of her grief, and someone she didn't even notice at first kept handing her the handkerchiefs into which she wept and wept. He never identified himself. He left it up to her to decide who and what he was when at last she came out of her sorrow. Of course he couldn't possibly be what everybody else said he was, the puffed-up midget who dared to smuggle himself into her heart because he had nothing to lose. The vanity of her pain would never have allowed her to see him like that. Her eyes saw the Dwarf, but her heart saw the Prince who offered to suffer for her, to absolve her guilt and ignorance with attention unconditional enough to resemble love.

And now, the deeper the wedding party pushes into the night, the louder her mother laughs and shrieks. Brushett forgets himself too, tears off his tie and jacket, waves his arms as if to clear the room and starts a jig. Hey, how his short legs fly! How he leans into his drumming heels, his body rigid as a post from the waist up. How he flushes with pride as the room fills with cheers. He keeps bouncing around like an emperor on a set of mechanical legs. It's his way of telling everybody that he's pulled off one hell of a deal.

Oh, yes, it's a deal all right. Her mother agreed with Brushett that the most suitable gift for the children would be new shoes. Stella had her heart set on a pair of fashionable ladies' boots she saw in the catalogue. For weeks she could think of nothing else, and when the parcels arrived the day before the wedding and Brushett brought them up from the wharf, she felt a twinge of guilt for having been so hard on him. But her box contained a pair of boys' boots her size. She understood what she was told. She's was only a girl. She would never work on the Gladys II *even if she wanted to.* Brushett had no time for her and accepted her only as part of the bargain. She looked up from the boots she didn't want but needed and let her hate collide with the cold grey of his eyes.

This time it was the sound of the front door which startled her out of her memories.

"Is that you, Brian?"

"Hi, Mom."

Brian dropped the car keys on the kitchen table and went to fix himself some instant coffee. Poor Brian, she thought. Was it something she'd done that he never married? Now he was stuck with her and her bad heart, and he thought he had to take a break from his taxi runs every three hours to check on her.

"Take your medicine?" he asked, while pouring the hot water.

"Yes," she replied. "And what if I didn't?"

Brian drew in his breath, stirred the coffee too long and too hard, and everything stood still.

"I'm sorry," she said.

He nodded, sat down, and stared into his coffee. She sighed.

He lifted the cup to his lips and drank. Why was he still around, she wondered, but quickly reminded herself that she liked it that way, even if it was unbearable for both of them. *He's never grown up,* she thought. *He didn't know know how to leave the nest, and I didn't know how to teach him, and now it's too late.*

"Alma called," she said.

"What does she want?"

"Why do you …?" She stopped herself. What was the use? He was right. "She wants to stay a week."

Brian cursed. He demanded to know why he was never consulted. Why couldn't Alma for once think of others instead of only herself? Who the hell did she think she was, and why didn't someone straighten her out once and for being the selfish bitch that she was?

"Why don't you tell her yourself?" Stella asked.

"I will. I bloody well will," he shouted, picked up his keys, and stormed out.

The door slammed. Discomfort stirred in Stella's chest. She should be angry with him for being such a baby. Brian had never gotten over his father's leaving the way he did, without as much as a goodbye, a drunk who doesn't find his way home one night and ends up in someone else's house and bed. Brian waited for weeks. Every time they heard footsteps out in the street he ran to the door. They filed a missing person report, which appeared in the local newspaper. Bob Sterling, aged 36, five feet eight, 150 pounds, sandy hair combed back, last seen coming out of the drugstore at Rawlins Cross. Two months later he surfaced in Toronto. He promised to come home once he'd completed the deal he claimed had taken him there, but he never did.

Stella checked the time. Past 2:30. She'd planned to do some knitting for the Children of Nain campaign but decided to lie down instead. She made sure the front door was locked, closed the kitchen window, drew the living room curtains, and slowly made her way up the stairs to her bedroom.

The house was almost 90 years old, one of those tightly packed clapboard boxes that crowd the upper section of the old city. Over time, Brian had redone all of the downstairs, but the upstairs hadn't changed since they'd all moved in close to 40 years ago. Brian could come riding down the narrow hallway on his hobby horse, and it would seem neither out of place nor out of time. Alma could emerge from her room complaining that Brian had been through her things again. Bob could be crossing from the master bedroom to the bathroom in his undershirt, newspaper under one arm, cigarette dangling from his mouth, another hangover smirked all over his face. At night, when the children were asleep and she lay in bed alone wondering whether he was ever coming back, she'd listen to the house the way Jonah might have listened to the whale that swallowed him. In the dark, sounds take on odd shapes—bubbles, pellets, strings, and sheets; torn shapes; abrupt shapes; shapes of nagging persistence and pain, even of relief and surprise; the deep and hollow shape of silence; and one more on stormy nights: the shape of drowning.

They never recovered her father's body. No one saw what happened. They said he must have been swept overboard when

Brushett ordered him on deck the night of the storm. Stella refused to believe that he was dead. At night, kept awake by a huge hole in her heart, she'd hear him keening like a wounded beast crushed between the swollen layers of the storm. She tried everything to reach him. She prayed. She called out to him. She assembled him feature by feature—his forget-me-not blue eyes, the golden hair, the little cleft in his chin, the scar a flying tackle had left on his cheek, the strength of his arms, and, above all, his laughter. But it was never enough. The keening grew fainter. Every night she found it harder to remember the shape she needed to give him so he could free himself from whatever it was that kept him drowning. The thought that she didn't love him enough to rescue him desolated her.

Uncle Walsh was the only one who kept talking about the death, until Brushett banned him from the house. Aunt Mary sided with Uncle Walsh and stayed away as well. Her mother maintained she preferred it that way. Stella concluded she'd written off a huge part of herself, the part that had been swept overboard with the man to whom she had belonged. Brushett got what was left, something oddly less yet more essential, like a tree stripped down to a skeleton.

He also got Ben. Stole him. At first only Stella had known how to comfort her little brother and understood what he needed to hear: that their father was stranded on an island, that he'd killed the beast that lived on it and built himself a hut while waiting for his rescue, that he might take a long time coming home because all he had were his bare hands, his teeth, and his wits, but one day he'd make it. But Brushett took Ben down to his schooner and showed him how the living go about things with real ropes and knots, real winches and sails, real spitting into the hard, salt-cured air, and by and by Ben had lost interest in the island and the lonely shipwrecked ghost on it.

What could she say? To whom could she talk? All her mother wanted to remember was that she'd married Brushett so she could offer her children a better home and a brighter future. Couldn't Stella understand? Stella understood perfectly well. They belonged to Brushett now.

Brushett has promised Ben he'll take him on the next trip to Labrador. Stella's mother objects. Labrador is no place for an eleven-year-old. Nonsense, replies Brushett. The boy will make a fine skipper one day, and it's just as well to start him off early. He gives Ben a friendly pat on the back, but there's a hard edge to his smile they all understand. Stella waits for a comeback from her mother. How can she just stand there and bite her tongue? Say something, for God's sake! Tell him your children aren't for sale! But whatever Stella's mother has to say goes silently through her arms and hands into the dough she resumes kneading.

"Told you so." Ben grins when Stella runs into him outside in the yard.

"You told me nothing. Nothing you know shit-all about," Stella answers fiercely. She can't decide whether Ben has grown shrewder or more stupid. He thinks he can walk around like the men down on the waterfront, but all he manages is a pitiful, half-baked swagger. And he's taken to spitting even though he has nothing to hawk up yet. He's becoming unbearable, even their mother thinks so. Stella finally understands she's lost. One by one everything she's loved has disappeared or been taken away.

"Sook!" she hisses at Ben.

Ben ignores her.

"You won't last two days up there."

"You won't be up there to make sure of it."

Everything boils up inside her, all the misery, all the hate and loneliness and self-pity. A huge lump in need of emptying itself is about to burst. She goes screaming after Ben.

It wasn't the phone that brought her back this time, nor the front door, nor a dog barking or some other sudden noise from the street. It was the turmoil in her chest. Her heart was thrashing with pain. *Poor Brian*, she thought with surprising calmness. *I'm dying.*

There was no tunnel. Out of the dark that had closed in on her appeared the house with the fence and wrapped itself around her. She found herself in a room and recognized the table, the doily, the kettle, the stove, and all the other things. There was a large picture on the wall. Inside it a woman lay on a bed. She called her name.

"Stella!"

The woman rises. She follows her through a long blur of things happening and unhappening until she finds herself standing on the deck of a small schooner slipping into a familiar harbour.

She steps off the boat and walks to the far end of the wharf where Brushett stands all on his own as if he's just seen someone off. She shakes his hand and wonders briefly whether she's made a mistake, because she doesn't recognize him in his open, unguarded gaze. There's something they seem to want to say to each other, something they missed some other time, but his eyes suddenly fill with pain.

He bends down and picks up her small bag of belongings. They walk side by side up to the house with the picket fence she knows she'll recognize as soon as she sees it.

She takes her bag upstairs to her room and unpacks. She's crying and accepts she has to but doesn't know why. When everything's back where it belongs, she goes downstairs into the living room where her mother rocks herself in a chair, to and fro, to and fro. The floor complains, the chair creaks, her mother stares into nothing. There's no reaction when she bends down and kisses her on the forehead.

Five days pass like that, five eerie, silent days. Something's brewing, she can feel it. Day by day her own mood gets darker. Day by day she watches Brushett looking more lost, more forlorn. On the fifth day she sees his first tears. Her mother's eyes remain dry, but a savage despair is spreading deep inside them. The tension is unbearable.

At last she hears people at the door. They're coming, a few at first, then more and more until the living room is filled with them. They're all dressed in black, standing around and not saying much. Her mother, also in black, comes down the stairs. They leave the house and walk through the cold, clammy day until they arrive at the cemetery. There, surrounded by rocks and trees and ferns, they gather at the open grave and sing a psalm with thin, sad voices. When it's time to scatter her handful of soil on the coffin, she wonders how the hand that's holding her arm knew that she'd stumble.

No one must ever know, she keeps repeating to herself. It helps drown out her mother's wailing, the suffering on Brushett's face, the minister's empty words, the shattered triumph in her own heart. It helps her through the ghastly procession with her little brother's coffin back to the house, and through the unspeakable night of the wake.

Two of the women return on the evening after the wake. They lay out Ben's body so they can carry it back to his bed. Her mother enters and sits down quietly. After some time she starts to moan, her moans turn into tears, the tears into deep, retching sobs. Stella comes and goes with cups of tea that remain untouched. She's angry with the relentless grief which accuses her and from which there's no escape.

The doctor enters Ben's room shaking his head and leaves again an hour later looking worried. Stella enters and finds Ben alive, barely, but fighting the fever. She stays with him for days, washes him, talks to him, apologizes over and over—to him, to God, to herself—until he gets better. When he's well enough to understand, she confesses that she'll send him into the Guzwells' home knowing the children there have the fever. She wants him to catch it because she'll be angry with him. And now she's happy, happier than she can ever remember being. They pass hours upon wonderful hours talking, joking, playing.

It does Ben good. The dark shadows around his eyes are fading rapidly. Before long he can sit up in bed again without her help. Not long after that he's back on his feet. And then

Brushett comes and takes him away, down to the wharf and the stages where the men favour men, where they putter around in their stores, smoke their pipes and chew their tobacco and mend their nets and talk about things they pretend can be discussed only by them.

At last Stella understands that this, too, is the way it has to be. The hate which floods her heart has to be. The curse she wishes on Brushett has to be. The disdain she has for her mother's complicity, that too has to be. And so has her bitter loneliness, this self-pitying belief that Ben robbed her of everything she ever had and was meant to have.

And now that she's come to see this, she can hate and love them all because it will be all right. Soon she'll have done everything she still has to, and then at last she'll be all at one with herself again and with whatever it is that will be reaching out and calling her name one last time.

There were two topics he knew he had to cover with his speech to the business leaders seated at the tables below him. Opportunity and progress. Both were tricky.

The ashram in the foothills of the Himalayas flashed through his mind, the tropical trees with their foreign bird voices, the rancid heat, the constant state of exhaustion, the smug waddle of the saffron-draped guru as he took his seat in front of the devotees and infused them with the drip of his endlessly circulating thoughts.

Everything people want is an illusion, the guru had repeated over and over, everything that made life what people thought it was.

How he'd loved those hours sitting among the others at the feet of the master, his ignorance aching inside him. Like a compassionate millstone the master had ground their coarse certainties into fine dust, and it required absolute attention and stillness to keep it settled.

They were tender times, the hours after those sessions when the bird voices no longer seemed foreign and a new kind of alertness stepped out from behind the dullness of exhaustion. Happiness is dust, the master had assured them, and dust is happiness.

THE STATION MASTER'S SON

The snow came. It went. It came again. And then it lay around for weeks not going anywhere while street grime spread all over it like black fungus. And that's how April had arrived in the city: mouldy and rotting.

Noon traffic crawled around Cavendish Square. It was Tuesday, the day the club held its weekly luncheons at Hotel Newfoundland. Gus Squires pulled into the lot, parked his car, and walked toward the main door.

In his younger years, he'd scorned the club as a pasture for old and prematurely aging businessmen, a place to chew the cud of the past with all the others who'd either lost their steam or never had it. Yet here he was so many years later, his membership badge waiting for him inside. Phonse Power, whom he couldn't stand, was coming up behind him in his silver Cadillac. Just ahead, Bernie Thistle was shuffling through the main entrance with a lecherous tilt of the head toward the young woman who was holding one of the glass doors open for him. Squires had the sensation of being pushed and pulled at the same time, just another car in an arriving train. He had an excuse, he told himself. He was young then, he was old now, and things change.

He was late. The meal—a pink granite slab of salmon, a forest of broccoli, boulders of baby potatoes, a driftwood of carrots, a milky sea of dill sauce—was well under way. He had just enough time to find an empty seat and butter a roll before the guest speaker rose from his chair at the head table, walked to the lectern, and waited for the applause to die down.

Andrew Cummings was his name. A young intellectual who seemed to be the latest favourite on the city's rubber chicken circuit, approved by some as an original voice, dismissed by others as a mere stage performer who produced ideas like coins and scarves he pulled from the sleeve of his tricky mind. He'd been asked to speak on 60 years of confederation with Canada.

"Believe me," Cummings began, "I had nothing special in mind when I decided to title this talk 'The Business of Progress.'"

Chuckles rippled through the room.

"So what is it you want from progress?" Cummings continued. "I suspect—but please feel free to correct me—I suspect it's opportunity. And what do you want from opportunity if not more progress to offer you more opportunity?"

A cramp of hate seized Squires. They were an incontinent bunch, these young pundits with their certainty that there was an explanation for everything if you kept talking long enough.

They treated every topic like a hydrant, pissed their thoughts all over the place, invented a whole new type of expertise which had them roam the streets of public debate and keep on pissing. They were the first truly displaced generation, and they didn't care because they didn't know any better. Just about everything that had mattered back then when people waged civil war in their hearts over confederation no longer existed. Every argument against joining Canada had been paved over by progress. Now that you could buy mangoes and papayas year-round at the nearest supermarket and it took only a few months rather than a few years for the latest trends from other part of the world to get here, who still knew enough to care? And how could you possibly care if you were a child of the highway generation, if you never had to step off a wharf to go see a doctor or board a train to visit relatives in the city? A lot of people lost everything because of confederation. Just as many made a killing with it and were still at it today. All you had to do was look around the room and size them up, these well-fed, well-housed, well-banked gentlemen of the local business community. Ask Bernie Thistle how he had made his millions. Ask his sons how they made even more, those paragons of progress and opportunity!

    He pictured his father in his station master's uniform, receiving and sending off trains like a traffic cop in the land of dragons, unfazed by the wrath and steamed-up metal, the hissing and fuming and grinding and shuddering on the platform. Yes, his father had believed in confederation, had welcomed the progress it promised and never tired of pointing out how superior diesel was to steam, how new communication systems would make transportation so much more manageable and efficient. As a boy Squires had stood in awe of this man who was never lost for perspective, and he grew up knowing that one day he'd fight for progress just like him.

Bernice Fowlow, who owned several fast food franchises around the city, gently tapped him on the arm and asked him in a whisper to pass the butter. He obliged without taking his eyes off the guest speaker.

"Let's get one thing straight about confederation," Cummings said. "You can't take a society where you think it should go. There's no such thing as a collective destiny you can drive like your car. There's only the natural course of things, and it's that which sets you free. Free to take opportunity in one hand, progress in the other. Free to start juggling."

Freedom and juggling! What did this boy know about either? Squires's own future had come up formally on his 16th birthday. His father declared it to be law and the civil service. There won't always be trains, he explained. There won't always be trees to cut or fish to catch, but there will always be government. The announcement struck Squires like a train itself. All the perspective his father had dished out while whistling progress in and out of his station had been no more than a fortune cookie with a note inside saying *Sorry*.

Squires hated every moment he spent as the station master's son studying law alongside the heirs of rich merchants. Later he hated all the small and sometimes not so small indignities of his junior position in a new provincial civil service still run by the old guard.

And then Adam Bennett came along. Everyone around the government buildings had a story to tell about the man's brilliance and his meteoric rise to the top of the civil service. The best story though, with all its variants, was the one about his sudden departure—his fall, according to his enemies. It championed what most knew, but couldn't say too loudly, that plodding was and would forever be the name of the bureaucratic game, that the old guard would always run the place like some universal constant.

Bennett had contacted Squires with a written invitation to meet him for lunch at the old Hotel Newfoundland. And there, in less than half an hour, he'd laid out what government planners could only trot out as long-winded projections: the future. Afterwards he took him on a tour of the city. He showed him the stench and clutter of the harbour, the clapboard slums around Brazil Square, the scores of unpaved streets that led nowhere, the whole dismal quaintness of a world he declared finished.

There was a new war on the go, he said. Could Squires guess what weapons it was being waged with? Squires shook his head. Asphalt and concrete, Bennett replied. He added that he'd taken notice of Squires and invited him to join.

So they built the roads and laid the pavement that led to the closing of scores of railway lines and junctions, including his father's. The old man never complained about it. He retired on a small pension, bought the house in which he'd lived as a station master, and took to gardening along the tracks where the trains no longer passed.

"I put you out of business." Squires once tried to open the subject.

"I sent you away." The old man closed it again.

Gerry Nolan clearing his throat next to him brought him back to the room. At the lectern, Cummings reached for a glass of water and drank slowly, as if gathering his thoughts for one final onslaught.

"So," he concluded. "Was confederation inevitable? Well, in hindsight everything's inevitable. But that doesn't mean you can't have influence. You can have influence by adding your own sense of must, your own priorities, if you wish. You can drift, or you can strike out and swim. If enough people think you're swimming toward something of interest, they'll follow, and there you are, something's shifted. Maybe there'll be a new opportunity. Maybe some progress. And maybe more opportunity."

The room erupted in applause.

A biting chill hit Squires in the face as he stepped outside. A cab pulled up. He waved it on impatiently and braced himself to cross the lot to where he'd parked his car. How they'd gushed over Cummings! How they'd lined up to shake his hand, to touch, no, to caress him with compliments. And yes, Squires had spotted it, the vanity in the boy. Too much piss. Far too much piss.

The sky was streaked with darkly roiling clouds. A few snowflakes swirled. From downtown came the pounding of a machine driving pylons into the harbour bottom for a new offshore supply base. His machine. Well, his company's. He stopped and listened, then remembered there was a small business matter he'd hoped to discuss with Ab Puddester; plus he'd meant to put his name down for the committee that was supposed to review the club's scholarship program. He turned to walk back toward the hotel just as Cummings came out still surrounded by a small group of admirers.

"To hell with it," he muttered, and fished for the keys to his car.

―――――――

Everyone knew the story, but the host of the open-line radio show repeated it anyway.

It starts with a huddle of houses, wharves, and stages at the end of a gravel road leading to one of those places of nowhere along the northeast coast that still calls itself an outport. The nearest school is a 45-minute bus ride away. Just before you reach the cove, there's a pond blocked with life from spring to fall and blanketed by ice and snow in winter. A range of hills dominates the view facing the land. Looking out to sea, the place is all sky and water and, on clear days, one hard line in between.

About a mile up the coast is the abandoned home of a man who spent half his addled life building a boat he was going to sail across the Seven Seas. He's been dead for years, but the boat is still falling apart in his yard. A flock of crows drops by early each morning and again at sunset. The boy often makes his way there after school and listens in on the unfulfilled dreams that spook inside the cracked hull.

The roar of the coral reef it never struck.

The howls of the jungle it never reached.

The pounding it never took trying to round Cape Horn.

But something about the carcass of that ship tells the boy that the world is worth saving, and many years later he will tell those who want to hear his story that this was how he discovered his destiny as an environmental activist.

"Destiny?" a caller to the open-line show jeered. "What

does an opportunist like Gord Pike know about destiny? Is that what destiny has come down to—making a damned good living from shit-disturbing at the expense of people who're just trying to make an honest living fishing and sealing?"

The open-line show host cleared his throat to say something. The caller kept ranting.

"What's his claim to fame anyway? So he hung out with a beaver in that pond, if you believe that cock-and-bull story. I have all kinds of wildlife in my house, like flies and spiders and carpenters, I hang out with. That doesn't make me an environmentalist. He's a traitor, that's what he is."

"I'm not sure I'd go that far," the host interjected.

"Well, I do," the caller shouted. "What business has he got to make us all up here look like a bunch of savages?"

"Turn that thing off, will you?" the old man said to his wife, who was knitting by the radio.

She dropped her needles and looked at him as if he'd told her to vanish. "Someone's got to speak out."

"That's just the problem," the man said. "Everyone thinks they've got to give their cent and a half these days. There's no telling what's up and what's down anymore."

"What's it matter if you know your own mind?"

The wife resumed her knitting. The man grunted, heaved himself out of his chair, walked over to the radio, and turned it off.

"Bunch of arseholes," he growled, as he left the room.

NEWS IN THE HARBOUR

A white van with a TV crew pulls up first.

A ship's horn goes off. It's impossible to say where. Even on the quietest days, the harbour is a huge mouth clanging and banging and throbbing gibberish into the sky.

A black minicruiser comes speeding down the harbour apron painted with the logo of yet another TV station.

It's mid-morning. The sky's overcast. A chill blows in from the Narrows. The usual flock of gulls is feeding on the bubble of raw sewage that wells up day and night off Harvey's Wharf, circling, diving, gulping, circling again, and screaming.

Joe Peddle wrinkles his nose. A toilet, that's what the place has come down to. No floating offal from the fishing stages that have disappeared a long time ago. No scraps from all the other old ways that have gone as well. Just the city's daily output of shit pumped straight into the harbour. And that, too, will be taken care of once the new sewage treatment plant gets up and running in a few years. Then it will be, sorry gulls, we've cleaned up and you're out of luck. Go eat at the dump! And some day that will be cleaned up as well. That's what humans do best, make a big mess and an even bigger fuss over cleaning up when it's already too late.

A subcompact carrying the logo of the local newspaper pulls up. A tall burly fellow gets out armed with several long-barrelled cameras he carries like minibazookas.

Peddle sucks up his hangover, gets off the bench from which he's been watching, and moves in as more media types arrive, all gathering next to the gangplank of the ship that docked overnight at Berth 10, just behind the Russian factory-freezer trawler. She's a small cargo vessel with a grey hull and a white bridge. Her name's splashed across her bow with bold red letters like a smear of blood.

Pandora.

A yellow cab delivers two men whom Peddle recognizes as local lawyers. He went to school with one of them. They nod as they pass the media huddle and make their way up the gangplank. Two crew members unglue themselves from the railing and escort them inside. No one on the wharf makes a move.

And then a tall lean man in jeans and a khaki combat jacket comes down the gangplank followed by the lawyers. Thick ash-blond hair, lawless blue eyes, long-fingered hands—the whole go-kiss-my-ass package. He walks up to the reporters. Microphones meet him like a gaggle of riled geese.

"We're not the pirates," he declares, in answer to a flurry of questions. "The ones who rape the unprotected, those are the real pirates."

"Hey Peddle! What's up?"

It's Ned Carter with whom Peddle had gone drinking the night before. He looks rough, unshaven, eyes bloodshot.

"Dunno. That crusader, I guess."

Carter runs the information through his mind, grinding it slowly.

"So she's come in, eh? Anything happen yet?"

"Nothing."

"Cool bugger," Carter whispers into Peddle's ear, his breath rancid from the previous night's drinking.

"Piss off, Carter. I'm trying to listen."

"We help those who can't help themselves," the man in the jeans and combat jacket continues. "All the unprotected species which have as much of a right to exist as we have, every bit of life that's on the hit list because there's no charter of rights to protect it."

Carter's face coils into confusion. "What's he saying?"

"He's telling them to kiss his ass."

"Proper thing."

"Captain. Did you or did you not try to ram the shrimp vessel?" The question comes from a reporter young enough to be a high school student. She has a sweet voice and is still innocent enough to use it.

"Why don't you ask the people from Fisheries and Oceans? They're the ones who are laying the charges against me."

"Then how would you describe what happened out there?" a

middle-aged blonde cuts in with a hard, knowing smirk.

"There are times when you have to become an outlaw to uphold the laws that should be in place but aren't because certain people don't want them to be."

"And that's how you justify interfering with legal fishing?"

"That depends on what you call legal. There was a time when hunting witches was legal."

"Captain, how many fishing vessels did you see out there?" another reporter jumps in.

"Fishing vessels I don't mind. But that's not what's out there. What's out there are vacuum cleaners. And yes, I interfered. Vacuum cleaners don't belong out there."

"Last time you came to stop the turbot fishery," the middle-aged blonde speaks up again. "Before that it was the seal hunt. Now it's to protect deep-sea corals from shrimp trawlers. You come and go. You never stick around. What's really in it for you?"

"Well, it's not to seek your approval. I'm here to take issue with those who've deliberately left the high seas lawless so they can plunder them. Thank you."

With that he cuts the interview off, turns, and walks back up the gangplank tall, lean, and arrogant with the lawyers in tow.

Silence falls. Peddle steps back and scans the surroundings, the Battery past Harvey's Wharf, the Southside Hills across the choppy grey of the harbour, the shipyard and container pier over the Waterford River, Harbour Drive with its cliffs of brick, stainless steel, and glass, all muted by the cold leaden sky. Even the rumble of the city has frozen into meaningless static.

Two more cars arrive and park under the *Pandora*'s stern.

Three men in dark coats get out and go aboard.

"They're bringing him out," one of the reporters calls out.

"Why don't they just throw him in the harbour?" Carter hisses.

"What the fuck do you know?" Peddle growls.

"Who needs to know? He's got no business here."

"Jesus, Carter. Don't you get it? He wouldn't be here if there wasn't a good reason."

"Well, anyway. You coming out tonight?"

"Hell, no!"

The men in the dark coats reappear with the captain between them. The reporters rush to the foot of the gangplank and pepper him with more questions. Cameras flash and roll as if to eat him alive. He ignores them and gets into the back of one of the cars. Doors slam. Tires squeal. Then everything goes into reverse until the place is deserted again. Only the gulls are left, circling and diving into the bubble.

Peddle shrugs and starts walking toward Water Street. His insides are howling. He needs a drink.

"What's that you're reading?" he asked.

"The Last Cod," she replied, without looking up.

He put his magazine down thinking that sometimes she was far too caught up with trying to save the world.

"The last cod," he said with a sneer. "Who cares? You wait long enough and it's gonna be the last shrimp, the last crab, the last fisherman, the last this, the last that. Sooner or later everything's going to be the last one thing or another."

She ignored him.

"You know what?" he said, swinging his legs off the bed and sitting up. "It's gonna be smart shit-eaters like rats that'll make it and take over. And then there's gonna be a whole lot of firsts again. Rats with trunks, and long necks, and fangs, and hooves, and wings, and flippers. Next it'll be rats with long arms and funny thumbs and eyes close together in flat faces, then with super brains, and finally with their own story of how it all started once upon a time in a pretty garden where those that ate meat and the others that ate grass still said hello to each other and meant it."

"You're missing the point," she said, without taking her eyes off her book. "We don't have that much time."

He slipped on his sneakers and checked his pockets for money.

"I'm going to get a slice of pizza. Want one?"

"Hawaiian," she answered, turning the page.

THE NATURE WORKSHOP

Kevin Norris, a 30-something-year-old, medium-height bachelor known to his friends as Kiev because of his blue-eyed, pale-haired, and vaguely Russian looks, expected music when he turned on the radio as he pulled out of his driveway. There was noisy banter between two hosts instead, and a pitch to listeners.

"Hey! How would you like to win a trip for two to Marble Mountain? All you have to do is call and answer three questions. If we like your answers, we'll put your name in a box. The draw is two weeks from now. Call!"

A caller introduced as Max responded after the next song. He had a nice young-man voice.

"Hey, Max!"

"Hi."

"Who would you like to be marooned with on a desert island?"

"Oh boy! My girlfriend?"

"No, no, Max. That's not the way to get into the box. Try again."

"OK, OK. But I'm gonna get in trouble. Pam Anderson."

"Now you're talking, Max. Now you're talking. How about food?"

"Food?"

"Yes. What would you like to be on the menu for Pam and yourself?"

"Oh, oysters, I guess."

"Pam's a vegan, Max. But you don't fool around, do you? How about music?"

"That's easy. Symphony No. 1 by Gustav Mahler."

"Number what?"

Kevin switched to another, quieter station, but all the way out of town, past the strip malls of Torbay Road, his mind kept circling the hat trick on the island. Woman, food, music—Pamela Anderson with oysters and Mahler. Crude, but what else was this Max going to say. Florence Nightingale with chamomile tea and the Rolling Stones howling for satisfaction? A desert island was bound to be hell no matter what it came with. One night? Sure. Two nights? OK, two nights. Three nights? He rummaged through his mind but came up empty. There was really no appetite, not even for one night.

He turned into the country lane where the workshop was to take place and became suddenly aware of his surroundings. The fleshy reds and yellows of dying. The floating and drifting of autumn rot. The self-devouring orgy of another year ending. He felt the long rains come on, the drowning in browns and greys. Perhaps Mahler was the right choice after all.

It wasn't that he wanted to surprise them at the office with this weekend retreat he'd signed up for. No, he needed it for himself. How things change! They'd all been quite content in their collective office rut when Joan Middleton came along and changed everything with her unabashed new-age thinking. All of a sudden it turned out that Bob had been a Buddhist for the last five years but had never told anyone. Liz had been subscribing to a whole earth magazine called *Gaia*. Even Joe, the self-avowed redneck in their small group of friends, had kept a secret: his love of orchids and his commitment to the cause of preserving bogs and wetlands.

That had left Kevin with no secret, no special knowledge with which to set himself apart, as the others had done, and it bothered him more than he cared to admit. He found himself haunted by old childhood dreams of drifting aimlessly on an empty ocean toward some unknown destination which seemed to be adrift itself. The content of those dreams, which he recognized as utter emptiness, started spilling into his waking hours and filled them with numbing joylessness. Even the phone at the office rang with a dumb shrillness that made him want to cry. He developed trouble sleeping, lay endlessly awake into the early hours of the morning listening to the swelling and dying echoes of night traffic, the wind moaning in the trees, things without names slamming in the dark.

After weeks of paralyzing blues, he bought a stack of new-age magazines in the hope of reading himself out of the hole into which he'd fallen. It was a desperate move, but at least it placed him at some kind of a beginning, which was better than drifting on an empty ocean.

Down the street from him lived the manager of the local brewery who took his Labrador retriever for a walk around the block every evening. Kevin ambushed him one day armed with an argument he'd read in one of the magazines. The product of the local brewery was a mistake, he declared boldly. It wasn't what people needed.

The manager took his statement as an invitation to banter.

"Well, for something people don't need, it's pretty popular," he replied, laughing. "Sales are up, and our market research is telling us we're giving our customers exactly what they want."

That's just what he meant, Kevin replied, struggling to keep the argument straight. Industrial production was a way of making dead things. People were already leading dead lives, they didn't need a dead drink on top of that. What they needed was something alive, something that was never quite the same from one bottle to the next. The problem with the manager's beer was that it was all the same. It was brewed for consumers, not for real people. It wasn't beer at all. It was just another product.

"If you want to make your own brew, all the power to you," the manager laughed again and patted him on the back. "Remind me not to send you a courtesy case this Christmas."

As if to score the victory the manager had denied him, Kevin related the incident to his friends the next day while having lunch with them at the cafeteria of the government complex in which they worked.

"What the breweries are doing is like stripping bogs and turning them into perfect lawns," Joe responded. "And then what happens when everything that comes with bogs is removed, when the taste of decomposition is gone? People get chemically concocted abstraction and the taste of everything missing."

"That's what happens when you go after consistency and use machines for it," said Liz. "It's chi that goes missing. Life force."

"Hey guys!" exclaimed Bob. "What do you expect? A brewery isn't a social institution, it's a business. If you want to drink the real thing, drink life!"

All Kevin could hear the rest of the day was laughter in his back. How they'd beaten him at his own game! Reading a pile of magazines wasn't going to get him anywhere. He needed an experience. So when he saw the ad for the workshop on the community board of his neighbourhood supermarket, he knew it was meant for him.

He passed the granite outcrop he'd been told to look for. A few hundred yards farther on was a wooden sign with a carved inscription. He had no idea what it meant, but there was no doubt about its purpose of putting visitors on notice that here was a place with special knowledge.

"Hi, I'm Laura. Please come in," the hostess greeted him. She was lean, fit, and attractive, but also as unrecognizable as if she belonged to a different plane of existence. There was something as hard as flint about her. He sized up the pile of shoes in the porch and guessed he was neither first nor last.

"There are still a few more people to come," Laura confirmed. "Make yourself comfortable. There's tea and muffins. If you want, there's coffee as well." By her tone he could tell that the coffee was a concession to people with bad habits. Still, the cup he poured himself was surprisingly strong and good.

He found himself in a large room with various sitting and meeting areas at one end and a kitchenette and dining arrangement at the other. About half a dozen people had already turned up. After the arrival of another half dozen or so, Laura called them all to order in a large circle.

"I assume you all know who I am," she said. "I know who you are. But I'm not sure you all know each other. So let's introduce ourselves."

Kevin shifted uneasily. They all made it sound so simple to state who they were and what they expected to get out of the workshop. By the time his turn came, his heart was in his throat. He had to stop in mid-sentence and swallow. He could hear the wheels turning in their heads. Who was this idiot? What was he doing here? And was he trying to be cute by saying he suffered from too much city?

Laura pointed at a basket in the middle of the circle. It was filled with small rocks.

"I want each of you to pick one of them," she said. "Identify with it because it's going to be yours for the weekend. And don't think of it as a pet rock but as a companion. Maybe by tomorrow afternoon you'll even see it as a friend."

Bodies leaned forward. Hands descended. By the time Kevin made his move, he was stuck with a plain grey, roughly egg-shaped pebble. Seeing the others fondle and caress their stones like pets they'd adopted with instant love despite Laura's caution, he hastily put his into his pocket. That's where it belonged.

They started off by learning about the medicine wheel, then about the wider meaning of colours. They heard endlessly about spirituality and reconnecting with nature, which, they were told, meant reconnecting with themselves. That, Kevin could have announced there and then, would take him more than just one weekend. He had no memory of ever disconnecting in the first place.

They toured the grounds with its wood trails and a small waterfall. After lunch, there was more talk about animal spirits and totems and the infinite connections, ramifications, and re-connections of the great web of life. Then, before the mid-afternoon break, Laura told them to go back out and find a spot to claim as their own. They had 40 minutes.

"You might meet some squirrels," she said. "Don't be afraid to communicate with them. There are foxes as well. If you happen to run into one, let it introduce itself first. They're very fussy with strangers."

He was one of the last to leave the house. A young woman had chosen an old tree stump barely 50 feet into the woods. She sat on the ground, absolutely still, her eyes closed, her face as timeless as a mountain lake. A grandmotherly woman with the aura of a lioness had found her place in a small hollow she filled like a statue. A middle-aged woman had positioned herself below the waterfall, pleased with herself for having picked a premium spot. A man with a short, red beard perched on a rock above the waterfall as if he ruled the world.

Kevin continued along the path until it ended at the foot of a rocky bluff. He turned, feeling discouraged. The more he looked for a spot of his own, the more he saw only those already taken. He came to the end of another trail and looked out over the forest rolling away into the distance, hill stacked upon hill in fading shades of autumn-mottled greens and blues. There were small clusters of houses here and there along hidden roads and lanes. He imagined them as places where fences were left to lean, dogs to bark on chains, car wrecks to rot in backyards. A shiver of fear ran through him, a dread of getting lost and never finding his way back again. He fumbled for the rock in his pocket. It felt ridiculously like asking for help.

The mid-afternoon break was well under way by the time he got back to the house. The carrot cake was exquisitely rich and moist. The coffee tasted even better than it had in the morning. Everyone was relaxed, exchanged trivia, talked about the fine weather, about late-season garden chores and pets and children and the downtown sewer construction project which had caused traffic disruptions along the St. John's harbourfront all summer long. After about 10 more minutes of that, Laura clapped her hands and called them back into a circle.

"So, how was it?"

They all smiled and exchanged knowing glances.

Laura turned to Bill, the man with the red beard, and nodded. He cleared his throat.

"Well, I knew right away that the top of the waterfall was the place for me. It was the water rushing by. Yes, that's what it was, the energy. At one point I felt the whole universe draining through me."

Laura smiled at the young couple sitting next to him.

"We picked a spot together," the woman, whose name was Lisa, said, blushing.

"We just got married," Bart, her man, explained.

A flurry of applause and congratulations followed.

"We didn't start out looking for a place together," Lisa continued, "but then we saw the twin birch by the brook not far from where Bill was sitting, and we knew that was it. It was like it was meant to be."

Everybody agreed it was.

Next came the young woman who'd introduced herself as Debbie in the morning but hadn't said much since. She looked down at her hands as if waiting for something to appear in them.

"I looked everywhere," she said finally, with a tremor in her tiny voice. "I couldn't find anything." She bowed her head and choked back tears. "I'm sorry."

"My God!" Laura exclaimed. "That's perfectly OK. The point of sending you out there was so you would open up. If that meant you didn't find what you were looking for, that's all right, my dear. That's quite all right. You know, sometimes finding is not finding. Thank you for that, Debbie. Thank you."

Debbie smiled uncertainly, then looked down into her hands again. Kevin imagined them filling with secret petals of pride. It was OK to fail. All he had to do now was tip his hat to Debbie and say, yes, the same had happened to him. Who knows, perhaps his spot was simply somewhere else, on some other property, maybe a plane trip away, a broken dream, 10 more years of getting older, another life, another planet. He knew exactly what he was going to tell them.

The woman who'd ended up by the tree stump finished saying she'd wanted a place that made a simple statement.

The lioness of the grove said the soft gurgling and trickling of the stream at her feet had reminded her of fairies she'd once encountered as a child. The woman from the waterfall spoke about fulfillment. Someone else mentioned the intoxicating reds and yellows of a young maple tree. And then it was his turn.

Yes, he couldn't find a spot either, he said, though he couldn't bring himself to look at Debbie as he spoke.

"I kept looking and looking till I came to the end of the trail, and that's when I realized I'd already found what I was looking for. I'd been on it all along. It was the trail itself. That was my spot."

He'd meant every word of it but felt like an impostor all the same.

"Well," said Laura. "That's very interesting."

He caught Bill smirking. Several others looked puzzled. Debbie shot him a dark look which exploded inside him like a grenade loaded with hate. His face caught on fire, his mind went blank. He had no idea what else was being talked about until he heard Laura call it a day. She thanked them all for having been such a great crowd and promised an even better time the following day when they'd explore some more ideas, and, yes, bond with a tree, and then tie it all together. He already knew that he wouldn't be back.

He made a quick getaway. At the intersection with the main highway he turned left, which took him away from the city through Torbay and onto Bauline Line.

He kept going. The houses petered out. Trees started closing in on either side. Ahead, the sun was setting in a pool of blood.

The road kept coming at him, the car kept swallowing it.

The car swallowed Debbie's dark look. It swallowed Bill's pretentious little beard. It swallowed Laura's invincibility. It swallowed all the others who'd found their spots. Slowly it swallowed everything except the little rock in his pocket he'd forgotten to put back in the basket.

All of a sudden he felt inexplicably and violently happy.

"The man has a problem, wouldn't you say?"

"I don't know," she replied. "It's likely that he has something, but it's not up to any of us to say what it is. It's up to him. If you really want to know, why not ask him?"

"I suppose I could, but I'm not sure that's the way to get the right answer. I doubt he knows himself."

"Of course he knows, though it's entirely possible that he won't be able to tell you. Telling the truth is never simple. It often depends on whom it's told to."

"And you don't think he would be able to tell me?"

"Well, you've already made up your mind that he has a problem, and I don't see what interest he might have in setting you straight."

"It might be an opportunity for him to set himself straight."

"You're right, it might. But I can't think of many people who willingly set themselves straight without a good reason, and in this case I don't think you're it."

AN OBIT

Eben White
Born April 28, 1943, Burin, NL
Died May 13, 2008, Dartmouth, NS

A light breeze ruffled Placentia Bay, full of spring and promise. The ocean sparkled all the way to the horizon. A gently sucking swell pushed and pulled the ashes away from the little cove into which we'd scattered them with two dozen white roses. Three of us perched on a narrow ridge of tilted bedrock and watched in silence as the grey slick that once was Eben separated into two halves. It was as if, released from torment at last, his spirit had decided to depart with a chuckle.

Eben had spent much of his life battling manic depression. When he triumphed, he was a lovely man—generous, unstintingly helpful, always eager to please. When the illness got the better of him, he was filled with hate and the helpless and self-destructive rage of a victim.

He died suddenly, though not unexpectedly, and without fuss. He had lived alone in an apartment building on the shabbier end of the Dartmouth waterfront, beset by diabetes, chronic back pain, and the black hole of his depression. He had once more gone off his medication. A friend had dropped in on him the night before and left him in reasonable spirits. Eben did not answer his phone the next day. Police had to force his door. They found him lying on the floor beside his bed. The officially listed cause of death was heart attack.

Eben and his younger brother, Josh, grew up near Burin in a small cove bristling with wharves and fishing stages. His mother was a seamstress, their father a seagoing rogue. It was not a bad beginning, but five years into Eben's childhood his father came home crippled by an accident at sea. And that was the end of love in their home. Josh left at the age of 16. Eben did not have the courage to make a move until he met his future wife, Pauline, four years later and she convinced him to move to Toronto. Mary, the older of their two daughters, was born at the North York General Hospital. Marlene, the younger, arrived in the back seat of a Chevrolet. They eventually moved back east and settled in Halifax, where I spent some years myself and got to know them.

Pauline, a red-headed, fiery beauty, was the great and all-consuming love of Eben's life. I wish I could say it ended happily. It didn't. His bipolar disorder was more than their intense and often stormy relationship could take. They separated when their daughters were in their teens. Pauline died of lung cancer years later, leaving a gaping hole in Eben's heart into which he descended time and again to look for her.

Eben was an extremely skillful cabinetmaker, a fussy and sometimes infuriating perfectionist, and also an astute collector of beautiful things which did not have to be of great value. He detested authority and had a sixth sense for the underdog. I suspected early in our long friendship that a big part of him—bigger than was good for him—had taken Peter Pan's approach to life never to grow up. Hence his enormous charm on the one hand and his terrifying tantrums on the other. Perhaps for that same reason he did not relate well to children, including his own.

He came to spend Christmas with us in St. John's three years ago. Once Doris, my wife, got over her reservations, she welcomed him as an unknown part of my life she would finally get to know. Our seven-year-old daughter, Tara, accepted him for what he was, a broken man with whose presence in the house she had been told not to argue even if it did intrude on sacred family time. He was perfectly behaved, gentle, almost childlike himself, so different from the raging husband and father who ended up destroying what he wanted and needed the most—the love and approval of his wife and daughters.

A snowstorm swept through St. John's and shut the city down the day after he arrived. We spent the day keeping a fire going, listening to an endless stream of carols, trimming the tree, wrapping presents, snacking on sweets, and drinking far too much sherry. By the time we were done with supper, there was nothing left to do. Doris put Tara to bed and retired soon after as well. Eben and I stacked more wood on the fire, went on the beer, and started talking.

I was surprised to discover how much rage was still inside him. Pauline, he said, called him about a year and a half before she died. They had been in contact on and off since their divorce. She was still living in the house they had bought when they first moved to Halifax, but she was not sure how much longer she wanted to hang on to it. One way or the other, it needed some work. She had heard that Eben was temporarily out of a job. Could he redo the kitchen? She would pay him, though she could not afford the going rate. Eben took the offer one step further. He disliked the apartment he was renting at the time. The lease was coming up for renewal. If she let him board with her, he would do the work for no charge. Pauline, letting an attractive bargain override her common sense, agreed. Perhaps she also rediscovered some tenderness for him now that the children had grown up and were no longer between them.

She was still employed as a secretary in a downtown office tower, so he was on his own while working on the house. He would make sure everything was spotless by the time she came home. She, in turn, was very good at cooking up quick and tasty meals. If she had nothing else on the go, they would make themselves comfortable, listen to music, play Scrabble, talk, or just read and be together. They slept in separate rooms. Eben was happy. She wasn't, but he made it his mission to change that.

He worked at it like a man patiently starting a fire with wet wood. Little attentions for sparks. Kindness for kindling he passed off as common courtesy. Agreeability for oxygen.

And all of it ever so discreetly because he knew she wanted no fire and would have kicked him out had she recognized what he was up to. That she didn't see it, or refused to see it, was entirely due to her selfishness. She made no secret there were times when he got on her nerves, when she wanted him out of the way, especially when she had friends over with whom he had nothing in common. But the house blossomed under his skillful hands. When the kitchen was finished, he tackled the adjacent study. When that was done, he turned his attention to the upstairs bathroom and the spare bedroom next to it. When spring arrived and the weather turned, he continued outside fixing the eavestroughs, repainting the entire exterior, then working on the roof where some shingles had started to lift and a leak had sprung around the chimney.

They went camping a few weekends that summer and slept in the same tent, and once they made love. Eben remembered a loon calling that night just a narrow beach away from their campsite. He also recalled that she coughed a lot. The cough continued into the early fall. She started to look drawn and tired but refused to see a doctor. And then she asked him to leave.

It confirmed what he already suspected, that she was sicker than she was willing to let on. He was convinced it was pride that had made her send him away, pride and stubbornness. She did not mind being spoiled, but she hated the idea of being dependent. That, he told himself, was quite understandable. He would look after her from the safe distance of living in his own apartment again.

It took him a few days to find a place and settle in. He called her number several times, but she did not answer. He left messages on her answering machine; she never replied to those either. She needed space, he told himself and backed off for another few weeks. Then he went to call on her.

Her younger sister, Marion, who had come down from Brampton, answered the door. What was she doing there?, he demanded. Even Pauline agreed that her sister was a user and manipulator. Pauline did not want to see him, Marion announced. Eben replied he wanted to hear it from Pauline herself. Marion told him to get lost and slammed the door.

Marion answered all his phone calls after that. She locked the door and closed the curtains when he stood outside the house begging to be let in. She arranged to have a restraining order issued against him. She called security when she found him weeping at Pauline's hospital bed. According to him, she also talked Pauline out of mentioning him in her will. That evening at my house, in my living room, only two more days to Christmas and its candle orgy of joy and peace, Eben bared his heart, and I could no longer tell love from hate. No one was spared. Not his parents. Not his brother who had done well for himself in Vancouver. Not his children, who had fled him. Certainly not Marion. Not even Pauline, who had allowed her sister and her own selfishness to come between them.

I know very little about Pauline's final days. Mary once recalled that her mother was in great pain and heavily sedated but rejected all sympathy and pity to the end. Again and again she would become agitated and ask someone unseen to leave her alone. Mary believed she was pleading with Eben. Eben insisted the persecutor was Marion. I never spoke to Marion about it, but I think she would have pointed back at Eben. I have often asked myself whether final accounts can be that simple, and perhaps Pauline was pleading with all of them, including herself.

In the last few years of his life, Eben finally did find what he needed among a small circle of friends who accepted him as he was and took care of him as his health began to deteriorate and his will to live left him.

He wanted his ashes scattered near the place of his birth, in a little cove where he and Josh used to play as boys. His daughters and Josh wanted nothing to do with it, so he came home alone, an urnful of ashes in my hand luggage. Doris, Tara, and I picked a sunny weekend in late June and headed down the Burin Peninsula to find the spot he had specified on a little map lovingly drawn by him.

One of the two halves into which the slick of his ashes had separated ended up larger and with more roses. If his departing spirit meant us to guess which of the two represented which side of him, I want to believe that in the end his good side came out on top, that somehow his heart, no matter how badly wounded, had prevailed. If so, it was no easy victory.

Some years before his cancer killed him, Vince Malone came up with the idea that, instead of looking for the most beautiful tree to cut for Christmas, he and his family should go looking for a Charlie Brown tree.

"Beauty is easy," he said. "Ugliness takes courage, and that takes imagination."

His oldest son, Ed, picked the first year's tree off a cliff. It wasn't ugly at all but twisted like an artful bonsai.

His daughter Molly's tree the following year had two tips, one of them stunted like an underdeveloped conjoined twin. She'd spotted it by the roadside not far from their house. It wasn't ugly either; it had far too much soul.

The year after that, Paul, the youngest of the four Malone children, found his tree in a bog, a skeleton of eerie beauty, dead and bleached like bone.

By the fourth year, the pick was Ben's. Poor Ben. His tree was neither ugly nor beautiful, it was simply pathetic. Ed and Paul ragged him mercilessly. Molly said nothing. His mother was particularly tender with him that Christmas. Vince Malone kept reassuring him there was something inexplicably heroic about the tree.

Ben gritted his teeth. He'd taken the whole thing far too seriously and made a big mistake. His choice hadn't been courageous, it had been stupid. He would show them all the next time, but Vince Malone ran out of life and took next time with him.

THE CORONER'S LAST CASE

Douglas Tobin of 49 O'Leary Crescent died exactly the way those who knew him well said he would: in the death hail of a massive heart attack while mucking about in his garden. Even his widow agreed the ambulance crew had arrived as promptly as could be expected. The plain fact was that Tobin had gone beyond the point where modern medicine could bring him back.

And yet, and yet, Dr. Ulysses Philpott wondered, after his interview with Alma Tobin, the widow. His first reaction had been to give her all too obvious grief the full benefit of the doubt. But there was one troublesome detail: a large bruise on Mr. Tobin's left temple. According to the emergency doctor who'd declared him dead, he must have struck his head on a rock as he fell. But what if?

Dr. Philpott took his time walking home that day. He chose the Rennies River trail. He longed for the sound of running water and a few moments of solitude. Summer was coming to an end. Flaming goldenrod and pale blue asters were everywhere. He would officially retire by the end of the week, which was only three more days away. This, it had been agreed, would be his last case after 28 years as the province's chief death inspector.

He'd seen everything, but now that it was all but over it seemed far too little. The evidence of blunt trauma to Mr. Tobin's temple was entirely consistent with a bruise that could have developed even after the man had had his heart attack. He fell, he struck, he bruised, all while crumpling under the death-dealing blow to his heart. Why not sign off on that, let the widow have whatever peace she'd probably earned in all the years, and keep the volume down on his own retirement?

Dr. Philpott had a quiet supper at his house. Dora, his wife, was out for the evening, but she'd put a bowl of beef stew in the fridge for him to heat up in the microwave.

If Mrs. Tobin had done her husband in, she presumably had as good a reason as any wife who's been married to the same man for most of her life. Was she justified? Well, was any killing justified? No one could answer that except the killer and the killed. Since one couldn't talk and the other couldn't be trusted, the chances of ever getting the full story were slim.

A push at the right time? Dr. Philpott felt a faint but unmistakable rush of excitement at the thought. In all his years of dissecting suspicious deaths he'd never come across anything as remotely intriguing as the plots with which the murderers of crime writers finish off their victims. It had always been the other stuff. A husband gone berserk after too much booze. One drugged-up bum in a downtown rooming house stabbing another. An impaired driver pushing the speed of his vehicle beyond his control. The stupid stuff without an ounce of forethought. The only man he'd ever helped send to jail for what he thought was a blatantly premeditated murder was later set free as wrongfully convicted. Looking at it that way, it had been a freak show. He'd long given up hope that he would ever get the chance to help track down an equal, not just another loser. And here she was, Alma Tobin, and her husband dead with a big bruise on his temple.

He watched a special by National Geographic on a trip to the edge of the universe, then went to bed early without waiting for Dora to come home.

The autopsy next day confirmed that Mr. Tobin had, indeed, died of a massive heart attack. There was no evidence of bleeding in the brain. Dr. Philpott felt vaguely cheated as he wrote up his report. According to information gathered in the neighbourhood by Cst. Tim Burton, Mr. Tobin had been the bully of his street. No opportunity to pick a fight had been too trivial. Fall leaves blowing in from an adjacent yard, someone's cat digging up his flower beds, a dog barking two fence rows away, a neighbour mowing his lawn on a Sunday afternoon—for Mr. Tobin everything had been an insult to which he had to respond promptly and forcefully lest he lose what his monstrous ego construed as face.

Lesser circumstances had caused greater revolts in history, Dr. Philpott mused, than another rotten marriage pushing another wife beyond the point of endurance. But even if there was evidence that Mrs. Tobin had set off a chain reaction which succeeded in killing her husband by heart attack, a clever defence lawyer could easily play the card of self-defence after years of emotional, perhaps even physical, abuse. A compassionate judge might let her off with a suspended sentence. A jury might even acquit her. Abused women who strike back are not criminals, a letter to the editor following her acquittal might say, they're the true revolutionaries, the hands-on heroines who do the dirty work in a war of liberation that's been waged far too much from small offices run by activists who've never had a hand laid on them by anyone.

And then, quite suddenly and quite against his own wishes, Dr. Philpott remembered his retirement party of a few days earlier. It hadn't been his intention to bring up duty during his speech—he would have preferred not to have given any speech at all—but toward the end it had slipped out anyway.

Of course it was exactly what everyone had wanted to hear, that, after due recognition of his quirky nature and his well-known and still undiminished fascination with death and gore, he'd been a public servant like the rest of them. Donna Garland, who'd been his secretary for many years, remarked how time had flown, how the day she'd joined the staff as a maternity replacement seemed like only yesterday. Well, it was nothing like yesterday. It was layers upon layers of memories ago. So much had come and gone, entire ages of assistants and technicians, police chiefs, deputy ministers and other meddlers, and all the countless bodies mangled on ship decks and factory floors, broken and twisted in highway ditches, cooked by fat fires, washed up on beaches like decomposing puzzles. How could that be yesterday? And it had occurred to him that making a living of inspecting and certifying such wretched dying could only be justified as a nasty but necessary service to the common good.

So he'd mentioned duty after all. But it had also been a warning to himself, because deep down he wanted Mrs. Tobin to be as guilty as hell.

And yet, he'd seen so much death in his life. He'd begun to think a long time ago that it was completely overrated. There was a very good reason why people died, and it had nothing to do with whether they'd been good or bad and deserved better than to be eliminated. Death was simply one of life's ways of recycling limited material. Being eaten was one way to get recycled, but there was also death by other means such as sickness, old age, and violence.

It had simply been Mr. Tobin's turn to be recycled. And of course his wife had something to do with it; she had something to do with it the moment she met him. So what if she gave him a push at the end to expedite matters? Tobin had the death he wanted and deserved, and that's really all anyone could ask for. Because what was the alternative? That everyone died the same death no matter what the circumstances? Dr. Philpott preferred a world in which individual deaths came with the same kind of diversity as the lives to which they put an end.

He closed the file and pushed it across the desk. The shadow of a small regret came and went. It had been a lovely little fantasy. He'd even imagined it written up in the papers or reported on the evening news: *Retiring Coroner Goes Out with a Bang. Coroner Dunks Grieving Widow. She Fooled Everybody Else but Not Him.* Applause. Applause. Thank You, Really. Thank You Very Much, But I Simply Did My Duty.

Another little shadow came and went, darker this time with a faint chill of shame. Even on his very last case he'd allowed himself to be carried away. He hoped no one at the office had guessed, but they probably had. Very likely they'd expected it.

There was no reason for him to stay at the office. The decision had made itself, as it usually did. Mr. Tobin had died what he, Dr. Ulysses Philpott, already the outgoing and soon-to-be-retired chief medical examiner, could reluctantly but in all clear conscience underwrite for the record as a natural death.

He sat up straight. Over the years he'd developed a habit of slumping while at his desk. Retirement would be the start of a new posture. The gym membership was already paid for, and the personal trainer had assured him he knew exactly what exercises to prescribe.

He got up and walked up to the window to take what he realized would be one of his last looks over the hospital complex to which the office of the chief medical examiner was attached. The day was grey and overcast. A flock of gulls had found an updraft coming from somewhere inside the hospital grounds and was riding it, floating, soaring, swooping, circling with unbelievable grace. For all he knew, Mr. Tobin's departed spirit was one of them.

She was cute, this weather girl.

He wouldn't have minded meeting her—on the street, in a bar, in a fancy restaurant, wherever. She'd likely be on someone else's arm and wouldn't even notice him. The guy she'd be with would have her all tied up in an argument he was determined not to lose, and she'd be wondering what he was on and what she could do to rescue him from his own blather. He didn't deserve her, and she was only now beginning to figure that out.

Rain and fog on the Avalon and on the south coast. Mixed sunshine and rain in Central and on the northeast coast. Sunshine on the west coast. Snow flurries, sometimes heavy, on the Northern Peninsula and in Labrador. That pretty well summed up the whole bloody place on any given day.

She had a funny way of moving, this weather girl, as if she was a child again back in ballet class. Her mother was probably watching her as she had been doing all these years, still wondering how she was going to turn out, how many more boyfriends she needed before she settled down, hoping she wasn't going to be stupid like her and give up on a career in order to drive the kids to school and the pets to the vet.

She skipped one last time and tilted her head with a slightly mischievous smile. She was still smiling when a train of commercials cut her off, car after car after car.

Screw the product you've been using—ours is better!

Your boss can smell your fear—rub some of this under your arms!

If these starving eyes from another third-world shithole bother you—send us money!

We have a new environmentally friendly product for you—hop on the bandwagon!

And here's a sexy car for you—just hope the broad who's gripping the gear stick like you-know-what doesn't come with it. She'll make mincemeat of you!

And then the train was gone, and she was back, unruffled by the blast, not a hair out of place.

THE DOLLIMONTS

Peter Dollimont, who for many years held the chair of Maritime Studies at the local university—his role was to be the thinker laureate, to ponder everything of local interest—maintained that every story is a prison. We may think we can break free whenever our stories close in on us and make us suffer, but in reality there is only one escape. Death.

That, of course, is the oldest, the tritest story of all, the one about the pit beneath the cell of our life into which each and every one of us must drop when the time comes, whether we like it or not. Adele, the beautiful wife Dollimont brought back one year from a sabbatical on a Caribbean island, disagreed. Who was he to draw the line? she asked. Humans start off with the simple fact of their existence, and from there they move toward an infinity of stories both lived and unlived, both told and untold. According to Adele, death is not the end but the final liberation when everything becomes possible, including the total dispersal of ourselves—our homecoming—into the unimaginable plenty of stardust.

I think both were right because they were like two drops moving away from each other on the rim of a circle which must inevitably bring them together again. When and where does imprisonment meet itself as liberation? Where does the sun really rise and set? Where is London when you're not looking for it on a map? Where is your own place when you live in it?

"Who's looking in and who's looking out?" Dollimont once asked during a dinner party at his house which included his plumber and the president of the university.

"Don't be so abstruse," I recall Adele snorting. "That depends on what you decide to call inside and outside. You know perfectly well it's all one and the same."

"I don't know anything of the kind," Dollimont replied with a knife-twisting smile. "And neither do you."

It was one of those moments to which hosts are not supposed to expose their guests. And, being a rogue with good manners, the president raised his glass of red wine to the incomparable universe and its favourites, among whom, surely, it counted the Dollimonts.

I run a small publishing house which specializes in promoting local writing. About a year ago I received a call from Peter. We knew of each other but had never met. He paid me a few brief compliments on one of my latest publications, which was being talked about at the time, then he asked me to come and see him at his home.

I was a bit put out. I am used to people calling on me, not the other way around. He received me in his study and offered me an excellent cup of smoked tea. We spoke about the unusually fine weather until the subject was exhausted, then he came to the point. He had a collection of musings and essays and other writings on issues of local interest he wanted me to look at with a view to publishing them.

I said I would be honoured.

He shook his head. "They're not mine. They were given to me by someone whose identity I can't reveal. The author would like to be left unknown as P. A. Wenlock."

I searched my mind for someone with the name Wenlock. All I could come up with were vague memories of a geology class in my first year of university and a spectacular collection of fossils embedded in a limestone with that name. The rock had been deposited hundreds of millions of years ago in a shallow sea during a warm, possibly toxic period of the earth. It was a mass grave of trilobites, bivalves, nautiloids, jawless fish, and stalked sea creatures which must have swayed in the currents of that ancient sea like wildflowers in a field.

Dollimont smiled as if he had guessed where the name had taken me.

"I'm afraid P. A. is no longer with us," he said. "I wish I could tell you what happened, but I can't. P. A. simply vanished one day. But we have the manuscript, and it means a lot to some of us."

It was a completely unconvincing bit of fiction, but I accepted that Dollimont had earned the right to it. He was a man of well-known contradictions. Physically he was heavy-set and coarse, the type who blends in on any wharf or at any construction site. Mentally he was lithe and nimble like a dancer. There was a quirkiness about him people liked. His opinions were respected though often controversial and hotly debated. Liberals saw him as conservative, conservatives as liberal. Local socialists—a hard group to define themselves—would have loved to claim him as one of theirs, but he was too complicated a fit even for them. His favourite sport, he once admitted, was to take the other side.

From the size of the manuscript he handed me, I judged it would need a fair amount of editing. I had high hopes. Though an academic himself, Dollimont was known to be critical of the academic style with its flat and disinfected prose. The ultimate purpose of clarity, I once heard him say in a radio interview, is not to create more clarity but to help root out new mysteries. Why he had chosen me to publish whatever it was I held in my hands as I returned to my office that day, he did not say, and I did not ask.

I did not get to read the manuscript for some time. There was simply too much else on the go: a book launch by a competitor, a government announcement on the restructuring of provincial cultural grants which required my participation, the opening of a new production at one of the local theatres in which I had a small but not unimportant hand. I was also rushing my own latest project into print—another half-factual, half-fictional attempt to reconstruct a plausible story around the extinction of the Beothuk Indians. At last I found an empty evening, brought home Chinese takeout, opened a bottle of chardonnay, and settled in for what I expected would be a challenging but enjoyable read.

I remember turning away from the pale light of dawn coming through the window as I slid deeper into the couch to catch a few hours' sleep. Bits and pieces of the manuscript followed me into my dreams—the paper rose Dollimont had used to argue that man-made things are really nature's way of secondary processing; the dandelion growing out of a pothole at the bottom of Springdale Street he described as his first encounter with a miracle; the foghorn which used to sing to him when he still lived downtown among the daytime shopkeepers and lawyers and the nighttime bums and artists; and the pigeons cooing to him as he sank into his bed until he reached the dark and silent bottom of sleep.

I found it hard to concentrate that day. I was exhausted and hung over from too many words, too many thoughts, too many images. I cancelled several meetings and a dinner engagement and went home early. I felt as if I would never be able to be at peace again until I had figured out what to do with the manuscript.

Dollimont had told me to do with it as I saw fit. That, I discovered, was easier said than done. I found myself dealing with a collection of everything, from the sketchiest of thoughts to complete essays and stories. The whole thing struck me as a cross-section of an explosion from nothing to all with bits and pieces in the making everywhere, some fully formed but most still caught up in an endless kind of becoming. I had no idea what to make of it, what purpose to see in it, what theme and ultimately what name to give it.

Dollimont called me back a month or so later. He was planning a drive to Markland to visit the winery there. Would

I be interested in coming along? If I needed tempting, we could have a trucker's lunch at one of the gas stations on the way. I was not particularly busy that week. I also felt that I was in his debt, so I agreed to join him. He picked me up shortly after.

The woods and ponds on either side of the highway lay drowsing under a clear blue sky. There is something about the stillness of midsummer that mimics eternity, and it was eternity which rested over the land that day like an indifferent yet calming hand.

We toured the winery. We had our trucker's lunch. I waited for the manuscript to come up, but it never did. He dropped me off at my office and told me how much he had enjoyed my company.

After that I became a regular at the Dollimont residence. There were many dinners. I am not the most talkative, nor the most remarkable when I do speak, but Dollimont seemed to have developed a liking for me. He often asked me to stay after the meals. I accepted that he needed someone to listen to him and his ideas, many of which I recognized from the manuscript. If Adele had ever performed the role of the listener, she had withdrawn from it or grown out of it. I was his publisher, so I guess I was fair game. I paid close attention, convinced he was dealing me clues. If he was, I never picked up on a single one. Sometimes Adele would join us. We would open another bottle of wine and move back into the living room or, on fine nights, out onto the patio to soak in the night rumble of the city. I discovered that Adele could think and argue every bit as well as Dollimont; in some ways she could do even better, because she had more powerful instincts. I was torn between obligation, friendship, and envy. What I envied Dollimont most, I came to realize, was his wife.

Adele was quite a bit younger than Dollimont, well educated, gracious, and gorgeous. She was of Creole descent and had grown up on the Caribbean island of Grenada. Whether she was homegrown or had been sent away as a young woman to be refined in some college or boarding school overseas, I do not know, and never had the opportunity to ask. From the little I do know, she and Dollimont met while he was doing research with her father, a professor of geography at Grenada's St. George's University. I never heard the story of their courtship. In my more sentimental moments I imagine her a local beauty who had somehow fallen under a spell only an outsider like Dollimont could break. So he brought her back with him. She must have felt like a tropical orchid transplanted to a subregion of the arctic circle. They modified his house extensively to let in as much light as possible, but there must have been weeks and months each year when she wondered how much longer she could hold out in the thin substance of the north. I got into the habit of bringing her flowers, mostly brightly coloured bouquets, roses on special occasions. It amused and pleased her because it gave her something with which to tease Dollimont, who, like most husbands, had become complacent about expressing his affection. He did not seem to mind. That's what good friends are for, he said.

It was during those evenings that Dollimont offered me glimpses into his own childhood. His parents died in a car accident when he was still an infant. He grew up with his grandparents.

His grandfather was a civil servant of considerable promise but chose an appointment in Grand Falls over climbing the career ladder in St. John's. He wanted to be away from the city, closer to the island's vast interior. His true passion was the outdoors.

Dollimont recalled his grandmother's telling him the following story. His grandfather, then in his prime, had come home from being in the woods again. He had run himself a bath and called out for the tea and rum he liked to sip while soaking. As she entered the steaming bathroom and handed him the mug, it occurred to her to ask him the question that had been on her mind for years.

"Tell me," she said. "What's dearest to you?"

She knew better than to expect first place, but she wanted clarity.

He lit a cigarette and looked at the smoke curling from it. There he seemed to spot something intimate, much more intimate than the married life she was holding up to him. She recalled a smile on his lips, the smile of someone who's just sealed a secret little pact. Then he gave her the answer with a careful lightness that devastated her.

"Well," he said. "There's the outdoors, and then there's the outdoors. Then, for a long time, there's nothing. And then there's you and the family."

Everyone, at least everyone I know, has some sadness in their childhood. I could see Dollimont growing up a lonely boy in the care of two old people, both of whom lived in their own world of defiance. Under those circumstances the burden of identity would have been on him as he tried to figure out where he truly belonged. And perhaps that was what I had sensed and admired in the manuscript without recognizing it at first: the no man's land of a voice with no fixed existential address. I see this island on which we live as a place which, because of its own still half-digested past, is forever struggling for identity. There was no such quest for identity in the manuscript. It was in many ways the exact opposite, an escape from identity into an endless play of possibilities. It broke all the rules.

More and more often I started dropping in during the day as well. When the weather was fine, we would move from the patio to one of the lower levels of their garden which sloped halfway down one side of a shallow valley. There, among rock-walled terraces of flowering shrubs, roses, and creeping perennials, among gravelled paths and small flights of flagstone steps, I thought I saw what Adele had given up. I often wondered how she really felt about her choice to live here—as a failure or as a liberation.

It was on one of those visits that I accidentally walked in on an argument between them. Dollimont had asked me to join them for lunch. The front door was open. I took it as an invitation to enter without knocking. I'd come to the far end of the entrance hall when I heard their frustrated voices.

I left and closed the front door as quietly as I could. Then I rang the doorbell. Dollimont appeared promptly with a welcoming smile and led me inside. The table was set for three, but Adele did not join us.

That night it finally dawned on me. How could it gave escaped me for so long! P. A. Wenlock was the pseudonym not just for one author but for two. P. stood for Peter, A. for Adele. I felt I had found an important key.

Dollimont called again several days later to ask me if I wanted to come along for an outing to the provincial museum and art gallery. There was an exhibition which featured a large collection of local art he wanted to take in—some sculptures and photographs, but mostly paintings and prints. He had planned to go with Adele, but she was not feeling well.

It was a lovely mild afternoon in October. The air was unusually still. I drove to his house, then we walked the short distance to the museum. All around us leaves were raining down silently as if someone was playing with a switch. Dollimont talked of the city stripping and of how he was looking forward to seeing it naked, the bones of its streets and the sinews of its power lines revealed again, stark and functional without shame. He kicked at a pile of leaves and commented how ironic it was that the same natural changes that made the city strip made humans reach for more clothes. In that crossing of opposite paths, he said, lay the seeds of human culture and the destruction of the natural world. It was vintage Dollimont. I felt I could not let it go unchallenged and pointed out—as I knew Adele would have done—that many mammals grow thicker fur in the fall as well. Of course they do, he said, and laughed.

He was a strong walker for his age, which I guessed to be in the late 60s. I was slightly out of breath by the time we reached the steps of the museum. A bank of clouds lay scattered across the glass front of the building as if it had tumbled into a broken mirror. As we climbed the steps, Dollimont observed that the museum's permanent display started right there, in the reflection of the outside world. He exchanged a few pleasantries with the commissionaire on duty, then we bought our tickets and took the central flight of stairs to the exhibition on the second floor.

I like most of what has come out of the generation that has shaped the arts here since this place became part of Canada. I like its raw energy, its ties to the still breathing past, its refusal to be seduced into the anxieties and abstractions and boredoms of trendy individualism. I like its taste for real shapes and its basic innocence, which to me lies at the heart of all good art. Above all I like it because it still has the quality of common property. Not surprisingly, Dollimont had very different views.

"This place is a curse," he said, as we stopped in front of a wall which displayed drawings and sketches of the Gros Morne mountains by various artists. "Pride is one of the deadly sins in life as it is in art. And pride of place is the worst."

"Look," he continued, sweeping the wall with a gesture of his hand. "Have you ever noticed how few local artists bother with depicting people? It's all about place. Where's the search for the human condition in all of this? You can literally smell the fear of self-discovery, the dread that after all the old betrayals and sufferings have been trotted out once more, we are no different from the rest of the world—no more and no less, in fact, than the outsiders we despise so readily and accuse of snickering behind our backs. A bit more honest self-reflection might remind us that the foundation of our famed friendliness is no more than cruel necessity forced on us by stunted land and stinting sea and the follies with which we respond. But no, we're so used to this place staring us down, we mistake our submission to it for love. I'm tired of it. All of it."

I felt that he was being unfair, that he was demanding the impossible and should have known better.

We went to the museum's coffee shop and ordered tea and scones with strawberry jam and whipped cream. The harbour lay below us like yet another painting. I remember thinking reluctantly that Dollimont had a point, because what I saw that day was not substantially different from what I might have seen centuries earlier. All the city with its quaint streets and colourful houses, its jumble of roofs and chimneys and the odd cluster of modest high-rises could not distract from the basic, almost brutal, shapes around it—the cliffs and scrubby highlands of the Southside Hills, the massive rock gate of the Narrows, the barren crest of Signal Hill. There would never be enough city to undo these primitive sculptures. They were forever the first art, the first inspiration. But, unlike Dollimont, I felt that they were also the one genuine silver spoon in our cradle.

Dollimont's mood improved over tea and scones; mine, on the other hand, deteriorated. I had grown to like him. That afternoon I realized how much I could also dislike him. I was starting to tire of his relentless output of ideas, his self-indulgent imagination, his compulsive commentary on everything around him. Perhaps I was also tired of being his mascot. But most of all I was suddenly fed up with the game he had started when he handed me the manuscript.

We sat in silence looking out over the harbour. He turned suddenly.

"You're having regrets?" he asked.

"I'm confused," I said diplomatically.

He laughed. "Confusion and doubt are the royal road to wisdom."

I have always felt that confusion is a curse. It may be a privilege for those predisposed to clear thinking, but in most of us it is a symptom of muddled brain function. I did not need a lecture, no matter how playful, on the wisdom of insecurity. I told him so and knew instantly that it was exactly what Adele would have done.

"Quite so," he replied, without batting an eye.

A fine mist saturated the evening as we walked back to his house. Neither of us spoke. I knew the time had come to give our relationship a break. As we said goodbye in front of his house, he gave me an unexpected and affectionate pat on the back. An explanation of what he really wanted or expected from me would have been more helpful.

I left on a business trip to Toronto a few days later. Two weeks went by before I had even a minute to think about the manuscript, several more before I held it in my hands again. When I did, I knew exactly what I had to do. I had to return it.

I left messages on their answering machine and by e-mail but got no response. A few days later I ran into Joe Turpin, their plumber, who informed me that they had left on an extended trip overseas and were not expected back until the following spring. I was tempted to drop the manuscript into their mailbox. On second thought I put it my office safe.

Just before Christmas, Jane, my older sister, came by to drop off Nicki, her poodle, before heading south for her annual escape to Florida. I did not mind because Nicki came with a routine of daily walks I enjoyed and knew I needed. It was on one of those walks that I came past the Dollimont residence and saw the for-sale sign on the snow-covered front lawn. Several days later the sign was gone, and a few weeks later a moving van in the driveway was unloading the possessions of new owners. I admit I was upset but had to remind myself that I had been a full participant in this absurd drama.

I asked around. No one had any reliable information. The Dollimonts had been spotted in southern France, on a Caribbean island, on some beach in the Far East, in a Prague café, but no one could ever say by whom. According to one story, they had been involved in an accident while on pilgrimage to Santiago de Compostela; a related account placed the accident on the trail to Machu Picchu. After that I would not have been surprised to hear that someone had met them strolling across one of the craters of the moon.

Their manuscript has been in my office safe for eight years. I take it out once a year, usually around Christmas, and I have become quite good at guessing which passages were written by him and which by her. Between the lines I can always hear their endless argument over the question of whether life is a dead end or a free fall. Every year there seem to be subtle differences in the script. I do not know whether it is my understanding that is changing or the manuscript itself. I would not be surprised if it was the latter.

There are times when I hate them, when it seems that every rumour I have heard about them is true, when they are in all the places the rest of us would like to be but are not by simple, stupid, and life-denying default.

I see them in all the glossy magazine ads, the travel posters, the divine comedy pages of *National Geographic*. I see them in a tropical sunset over a palm-studded beach, a dark-skinned ferryman guiding their boat while bestowing on them a smile of unqualified approval. I see them with a family of herders on an Asian plain drinking fermented yak milk and trying to laugh their way out of eating roasted eyeballs. I see foot-scraping guides welcoming them to the Great Wall, the Pyramids, the jungle-infested marvel of an ancient temple. I see the Amazon, the wastelands of Patagonia, the misty slopes of the Mountains of the Moon, and I think how lucky they are, even if they are dead. They escaped.

BIOGRAPHY

Azzo Rezori is a retired Canadian journalist. He grew up stateless in post-war Germany, studied zoology in Ireland, and came to Canada as a post-graduate student. He experimented with careers in small engine mechanics, interior decoration, carpentry, and housekeeping until a friend, who knew him better than he knew himself, steered him toward journalism. Rezori worked for several newspapers across the country before ending up in St. John's, where he became a long-time and well-respected member of CBC's local TV newsroom. He lives in St. John's with his wife Brenda and their daughter Gaia.